The Disappearing Bloodline

by

Avis M. Adams

Lavender and Time

Cover Art by *Tina Lynn Stout*

The Wild Rose Press, Inc.
PO Box 708
Adams Basin, NY 14410-0708
Visit us at www.thewildrosepress.com

Publishing History
First Edition, 2026
Trade Paperback Print ISBN 978-1-5092-6445-2
Digital ISBN 978-1-5092-6446-9

Lavender and Time
Published in the United States of America

Dedication

To Amahle. You are the heir of all my stories, real and imagined. I love you.

Acknowledgements

As I release another novel into the world, I want to recognize all the amazing people I rely on as I draft, revise, and polish these books. First and foremost, to my critique group Flamingos Reborn: Carl, Catherine, and Melanie. Bless you all for BETA reads and all the sessions where you listened to chapter after chapter of this book, helping me rein in the wild characters and the unruly scenes! I couldn't have written this book without your input and support.

I'm also indebted to Debut22, a group with too many names to mention here, created by fellow authors at TWRP to provide support with ARC reads, reviews, and promotional tips. I couldn't ask for a better group of savvy writers to help me on this publication journey. Also to the friends I've made in Portland, like Allison who gives a kickass BETA, painful, but worth every rewritten scene to create a stronger, more meaningful story. To Molly, my friend and neighbor with whom I share many morning coffee sessions discussing the world of publishing and what it means to be a publishing writer in the 21st century. Thanks for your astute BETA that helped create not only a stronger story, but an antagonist worth despising or caring about, whatever floats your boat.

To the Baker Street Writers in Washington, who still let me sit in on the occasional meeting and graciously listen to my work. Your observations are always spot on, and I appreciate every one of your sharp comments.

And finally, to my editor Ally and her senior editor Rhonda for believing in my projects. They have seen me through five rounds of galleys and proofreads, and it's a pleasure to work with them on the publication of another piece of my heart.

Thank you one and all!

Chapter One

Aunt Eli was dead, and all her secrets had died with her. Sam put a hand to her heart. The Mount Pleasant Cemetery sprawled before her as she tried to focus. The funeral rites droned on. Had it been two months already?

"We commit your daughter, Elise Delores Allemande-Bruce..."

Sam's vision blurred as the minister's monotone voice continued. When would the shock of losing Aunt Eli end?

A warm breeze lifted tendrils of hair from her temples, and the dank soil filled her nostrils. She hooked her arm through Dad's, and he patted her hand as the minister read another prayer, this one in Romanian.

Sam leaned into Dad's side. Aunt Eli's strictness had been legendary, and she had imposed it on everyone, but she'd doted on Sam with smiles and her famous butter cookies. Aunt Eli, the "Cookie Auntie," had never been sick as far as Sam remembered, so her sudden death still hadn't registered. What did register was how much Sam needed her.

Dark clouds hung low overhead, but no rain fell. The ozone in the air left a metallic taste in her mouth. She leaned into Dad's warmth. He understood her shock. Dad's warmth comforted her. Mom, on the other hand, stood rigid on the other side of Dad, her dark hair pulled into a tight bun and every hair sprayed in place. Her bright red lipstick contrasted with her pale complexion and gray eyes. She was under the influence of her own emotional storms.

Sam couldn't worry about Mom's grief when her own was tearing her apart. Besides, the ever-present Archie needed her attention. He stood near the minister, his circa 1970s gold and tan plaid suit clashing with the smart black jacket of the religious man. Mom scowled at Archie. Was she afraid he would shift into cat form in front of all the guests? He'd never shifted in public before, but with his emotions running high, anything was possible.

Mom concentrated on the urn on the table before them as if communicating her displeasure to Aunt Eli's ashes. The move into "The Mansion," as she called Aunt Eli's house, had not been without its own drama. As soon as Aunt Eli was dead, and the will was read, she'd found herself packing boxes against her will. She'd threatened to replace all the heavy velvet drapes in Aunt Eli's grand turn-of-the-century monstrosity, as she called it, along with most of the antique furnishings.

Dad convinced her to hold off on any changes he wasn't emotionally ready to make. She'd overheard Archie imploring him to wait until he'd sorted out necessary furnishings with the "normal" furniture, which meant "magic." He was in shock. They all were, but Mom had become silent and brooding. Was that how she handled change or grief or both?

An older man cleared phlegm from his throat, and his elderly wife scowled at him. Aunt Eli's friends, one resting on a cane, two with walkers, a group of five hunched over and grim, congregated opposite the family to pay their respects. The minister had led them all from the reception room in the funeral home to hunker together under this covered area in front of the columbarium. Sam perused the wall behind her filled with names and dates on marble plaques, each one naming whose ashes were laid in eternal rest.

She turned with a sigh. The base of Mt. Rainier was all she could make out in the far distance as dense clouds brushed the tops of the foothills. Sniffles and low murmurs filled the air. Practical Aunt Eli would have wondered at all the crybabies and ridiculed Archie's tearstained face. Pragmatic to the end, she had no tolerance for sentimentality.

Archie never cried, in human form or cat form, for that matter. He only appeared in human form when the family needed him in his role as Protector. Sam had always known him as the orange tabby who sat at her Aunt Eli's feet.

Aunt Eli.

Sam pulled out her handkerchief and wiped her tears away. Aunt Eli would have laughed at her, too. And how much knowledge had she imparted to dad about becoming the next Guardian? Would Archie complete Dad's training now?

She patted her pocket for a Kleenex. Had she used them all? She wiped her nose with the back of her hand as Archie hovered beside the table covered with flowers. He ran his finger over the urn containing Aunt Eli's ashes.

A tingle ran down her spine.

A flash lit the sky, then thunder cracked in the distance. Hail dropped in a burst from the clouds, and she plugged her ears. The racket of hail hitting the roof was deafening. Archie shot a quick glance at Dad, who

3

nodded.

Was this tied to Aunt Eli's passing? Magic?

****

A crack of thunder rattled the window, and Nicole Blevins raised her eyes to the ceiling. How was she supposed to study in this racket? The living room couch and coffee table held her biology and history books, and papers littered the floor and side table. Hail hammered the roof. A dim light filtered through the sheers as she reached over to turn on a lamp. Nicole slouched back into the pillows and rubbed her temples.

She shook her head to focus. Only two more pages to go, then she could go to the movies with Sam, guilt-free. She leaned forward on the couch and stared at page 267 of her history book, running her finger over the same paragraph for the fourth time. What did the Stock Market Crash of 1929 have to do with her life?

Footsteps clomped up the wooden steps to her front door. She paused. Was the funeral over already? She frowned. Okay, so maybe she was behind in history, but she'd wanted to pay her respects to Aunt Eli, too.

The doorbell chimed. Sam never rang the doorbell. Nicole pulled her finger from the page, then jotted down a note before she forgot it. She had to ace this test, or it was summer school.

Again.

The doorbell dinged again. "Mom." Where was that woman? Ugh. She had to finish this chapter. "Mom. Door."

The chimes set off a third time, and Nicole tucked her pen behind her ear and dragged herself from her chair. Why now? She flung the door open. "What?"

The deliveryman gave her a blank stare. People must

give him crap all day. She ducked her head. He didn't deserve her anger. She gave him a thin-lipped smile, her attempt to cut him some slack. He held up a large white envelope with "AIRMAIL" stamped on it.

He stepped closer under the small porch roof as hail bounced off his wool jacket, then said, "Sign here." He pointed to a line on the bottom of a sheet of paper attached to a clipboard.

She stared at the paper. "Going old school?"

He held out the paper without further comment. She read: ROYAL MAIL: SPECIAL DELIVERY printed in tall red letters across the bottom of the envelope. She glanced back to the disgruntled man who held out the paper for her to sign along with the envelope.

She took in the disheveled man before her. Didn't they have a dress code at the Post Office, and where was Mr. Webster the usual guy?

"Mom. Mailman needs a signature." She waited. Where was she?

The unkempt deliveryman waved the paper pad in her direction again. "I'm not the mailman, and anyone can sign." His hat tilted to the side of his head. His rumpled brown denim jacket had a badge on the breast pocket that read *C. G. Delivery*. and his blue slacks had a sheen from what looked like French fry grease. Gross.

Nicole blinked. "Anyone can sign?" A sour odor preceded his outstretched arm, and Nicole scrunched her nose.

He nodded and smiled.

At this point, she'd do anything to get rid of this guy. "Okay." She pulled her pen from behind her ear and scratched out her signature on a dotted line.

He tucked the paper with her now streaked signature

into a pocket inside his jacket as he handed her the envelope, turned his back to her, and marched down the steps. "Have a nice day," he mumbled as he trotted into the hailstorm, seeming to evaporate into a mist.

Nicole did a double-take. Did that really just happen? She turned the envelope to check the return address.

Peebles' Pretties Toy Shoppe
44 James Street
Covent Garden
London WC2E 8RF

London?

Nicole rushed to the kitchen. "Mom?" She ran her fingers over the address. Rain pattered against the window, and basil from Mom's lunch lingered on the air. She dropped the envelope onto the counter. "Mom?" she called again.

****

Mist rose from the headstones. Sam scanned the blanket of grass as the priest recited the final prayer, and the mourners responded, "Amen." She swallowed her tears, lost in memories of Aunt Eli.

Aunt Eli had explained as much as she could about Portland, and Sam was beginning to understand, but how would she get over her fear of leaping through time with Dad and Archie avoiding her questions?

She chewed on her thumbnail. Mom scowled at her, and she dropped her hands to her sides. She was too distracted by the night terrors, the loss of appetite, her anxiety ever since that first jump. It all stemmed from those stupid bricks, and her fear of not understanding how they worked.

She wiped her nose on her sleeve this time before

shaking hands with an elderly friend of Aunt Eli's whose name escaped her if she'd ever even known it. Archie, as well, shook a hand or two, but he remained rigid, his shoulders back and eyes closed. What a weirdo. She had to put up with him, though. He was part of traveling through time, and the magic bricks, not to mention the scent of lavender which permeated the purple, velvet-covered book. Did everything have to be tied to lavender?

She blew her nose and squinted at the foothills covered in snow and Mt. Rainier gleaming through a break in the clouds. Steam rose from the grass as the hail melted as fast as it had fallen. Cosmic humor?

Thanks a lot, Aunt Eli.

Aunt Eli's musical laughter had always filled her with joy, but she'd never hear it again. She turned back to the minister, who shook hands with Dad, then Mom, then the small crowd shuffled to the road and their cars parked in a line behind the limousine.

Archie bowed his head as he stood beside Mom unblinking. Why hadn't he followed the mourners? Did he feel obligated to keep watch over Aunt Eli, even in death? He'd always preferred his orange tabby cat form and sleeping in the "throne room," so this must be difficult for him. She stared at his sleek ginger hair combed back from his face, and he gazed back with amber eyes, red-rimmed from crying. He was grieving.

With a sigh, she walked across the lawn to the waiting limousine, opened the door, and climbed into the back seat. Archie would be a big factor in what she learned about the family traditions and all the artifacts from now on, but Aunt Eli had been the only link she had with him.

Sam pretended to stare at her hands, but she was keeping sight of Archie from under her half-closed lids. How would she live with a shape-shifting creature she didn't trust?

Mom climbed in, and Dad sat beside her, forcing her shoulder to touch Archie's. She pulled away as the limo driver steered the car onto the cemetery road, and the procession of mourners followed them to "The Mansion." Sam sank into the plush seat as the sun broke through the clouds. Mt. Rainier glowed in the distance, and the hair at the nape of her neck rose.

Big changes were coming.

Chapter Two

Nicole stood at the kitchen counter gazing out the window over the sink. The sun broke through the clouds and glared off the deck. She picked up the envelope with her index finger and her thumb and held it in front of her. She'd better open it. She held it closer as she leaned against the counter beside the sink and reread the address.

Who could have sent her mail? Yet, her name was written on the envelope. She stared at it but didn't recognize the handwriting, then scowled at the address. She didn't know anyone in England. Did she? Maybe someone on dad's side?

She checked the postmark again. The time stamp said September 28, 1929. A shiver tickled down her spine. Wasn't that someone's birthday? Did she believe in coincidences? Since Portland happened, she believed in a lot of things, like time travel, for one. The envelope shook in her hands. What should she do now, open it? She sniffed it. Paper, dust, and was that a hint of lavender? She sneezed.

Light flowed into the kitchen, making the yellow walls glow in a cheery, bright light. A relief after the hailstorm. She ran her finger under the flap and tipped the envelope to reveal a smaller envelope, yellowed with time. The smaller envelope was already open. What did that mean? She pulled out a piece of paper yellowed with age and perused the envelope again. Streaks of dirt were smeared across it like it fallen on the ground. She read the address.

Miss Darlene Meyer

16 Lincoln's Inn Field

London

WC2A 3ED UK

Darlene Meyer? Like Freddie Meyer from Portland? One of her Greats was named Darlene, right? She shuddered. Was this another time travel debacle?

"What the hell? Get a grip, Nicole. Just read the damn thing."

She pulled out the fragile paper folded into a four-square and opened it.

Dear D,

I'm praying that this letter finds you before you leave. Pardon me for my boldness, but...

I am immigrating to America aboard the same vessel as your family. I will look for you on the aft deck every afternoon at 4:00 pm. I hope you will join me for tea. I have something of great urgency to discuss with you.

Your most obedient and ardent admirer,

G

"Who's 'G,' Grandma?" Funeral be damned. She pulled out her phone and texted Sam.

****

Sam trotted down the marble staircase that curved in a graceful spiral to the very depths of the big stone house. The "throne room" had been in the basement since she could remember. To Sam, it oozed magic with its stained-glass windows and granite fireplace, like a faerie castle. Aunt Eli had always limited the time Sam spent there, never letting her visit this sacred space by herself.

Sam had been twelve when Aunt Eli led her down the marble stairs and pulled back the burgundy curtains that revealed a vault door.

"Are we rich?" She'd turned to Aunt Eli.

She'd chuckled. "I'm afraid not."

"Why is this giant safe down here?" She ran her hand over the big, black metal vault with Barnes Safe & Lock of Pittsburgh painted in gold lettering across the front.

Aunt Eli walked to her and pulled her hands into her own. "One day you will understand what happened in Portland, but today, I wanted to introduce you to your legacy, your heritage." She swung her arm around to indicate the wing-backed mahogany chair, the matching mahogany table, the giant, ancient cases with locked, glass doors.

"What legacy?" She stood with eyes on the vault's silver door, the brick interior. She counted eight dead bolts and followed the contours of a complex locking system shining in the colored light from the stained-glass windows.

"You are almost a teen, and I want you to be familiar with what is to come." She sat like a queen without a crown, dwarfed by the size of her throne.

"With what is to come?" she'd asked, but Aunt Eli had changed the subject.

Sam glanced around the chamber. That memory seemed from another lifetime ago, and now she regretted not listening closer to what her aunt was trying to tell her. She brushed tears from her eyes. She missed the smile that lit Aunt Eli's face when Sam said something funny or clever.

This was the legacy she had been talking about, wasn't it?

She turned and ran her hand over the mahogany desk. It filled one half of the large space. Stained glass windows framed in white lined the upper edge of the south wall. They radiated hues of blue, red, green, and yellow light into the room. Was that a trick of light or of architecture? Sam didn't care. This space had always fascinated her. She plopped into Aunt Eli's giant seat. She bounced back to her feet. The springs, tight and buoyant, sent her airborne, landing on her hands and knees as if being rejected by the maroon chair.

A tall, ornate bookcase stood against the west wall to the windows. The marble staircase dropped into the room from the east, and the vault sat behind curtains on the north wall.

Aunt Eli had explained about the four directions. "The stairs enter from the east representing new growth and new beginnings, which is perfect for you as our newest indoctrinate."

She understood more about what it was to be an indoctrinate, but did that save her from the Portland fiasco? No. She stood in the center of the area, eyeing Aunt Eli's place of honor as though her ghost sat there. It had just ejected her. Had it rejected her?

She ran her hand along the edge of the map table. It stood like a stanchion of the space it inhabited, pulling all four directions to its surface: north, south, east, and west. Aunt Eli had explained that the design had followed specific parameters for the vault, which was twenty by twenty feet. Sam paced it out. Yep, twenty by twenty. She'd also explained the significance of "twenty" as "the balance of the body and the energy of harmony." All things important to time-travel, she was finding out, but that didn't make her want to transport across time. She'd said something else, too. What was it?

Oh, yes. "In Numerology, Two and Zero link partnerships, spiritual pathways, and collective energies." Also important in time-travel. She'd been oblivious the whole time Aunt Eli was trying to teach her what she needed to know. Archie was making a mess of it. How could a cat teach her anything? He did fine if it was by example, but he often didn't have the words, not like Aunt Eli.

The huge, mahogany table held a pile of books, stacks of old papers, and several maps, and Sam scanned them, stopping on one. Was it glowing? It seemed to pull her fingers to its edges, and she lifted it, focusing on the center. The scent of lavender hit her nose, and she placed the map on the table.

London, she read printed across the top. Covent Garden circled in red grease pen, and Peebles' Pretties Toy Shop in blue. She ran her finger over the winding roads and alleys, stopping on the toy shop. Her finger tingled, and she pulled it back. It wasn't hot, but it was too much like the tingle the bricks gave her, and she didn't trust either.

She stared at the marble steps opening into the room. Archie trotted down the stairs in his cat form and jumped onto a tufted foot cushion, the same burgundy as the other furniture and curtains. He ignored her as he curled into a ball with his head tucked into his body.

He might be asleep, but she still didn't trust him, and Aunt Eli wasn't there to supervise him anymore. She turned to the bookcase that ran floor to ceiling and wall to wall. It stood on the west wall because, as Aunt Eli said, west represented a move from ignorance to wisdom, and books helped with knowledge and wisdom. She grinned and glanced to the ceiling. "See? I did pay attention."

Carved mahogany Corinthian columns divided each section of the case and held up the arched top that was carved with floral designs. Four beveled glass doors with brass knobs locked over *The Tome of Truth* and other priceless books. Aunt Eli's Bible stayed in Dad's office upstairs in a matching case behind a locked door. Would Sam ever gain access to those books? They held the secrets of the magic, so probably not.

Dad was stricter at controlling the books and the knowledge than Aunt Eli. He never let her enter his office, and Archie showed up minutes after she'd come downstairs. Coincidence?

She thought not, but why was she curious and terrified at the same time?

Her phone chimed, and she pulled it out of her pocket. "Nicole?"

****

Sam walked up the front steps to Nicole's house and peered into the living room from the porch. Surrounded by history notes, Nicole sat cross-legged on the floor. Sam opened the front door. "Nicole?"

Nicole's footsteps pounded to the front door.

Sam pushed past her into the house. "So where—"

Nicole pulled Sam to the kitchen.

"Umm—" Sam stumbled over her feet, scanning the house for Nicole's mom. "Are you alone?"

"Mom must be at the store." She grabbed a large white envelope from the counter. "I received a letter today." Nicole exhaled as the scent of lavender hit Sam's nostrils.

"A letter?" Sam shrugged. "Okay."

"Do you smell it, the scent of lavender?" Nicole waved the envelope through the air.

Sam's shoulders tensed, and a familiar pain shot down her right arm. "Lavender? Like—"

Nicole pulled out a smaller yellowed envelope. "Just like Portland, which was not fun for me. I'm so sick of lavender." Nicole opened the envelope and pulled out a yellowed sheet of paper, holding it to Sam. "Read it. Let me know what you think it means because I'm freaking out here."

"Why?" Sam did not take the letter.

"I might as well be holding the ghost of my great-grandmother. It's too weird. It arrived near the day they departed for America, I think? September 28th."

"What?" Sam reached for the yellowed envelope and scanned it. "It's from 1929, and it reeks of lavender?"

"I know, right? Does this mean we need to use the bricks to go back to 1929?"

"Let's not rush to conclusions. We should probably show this to Dad. Its showing up here—"

"Isn't an accident, I know." Nicole shifted from one foot to another.

Sam handed the envelope back to her. "Agreed." She stood and grabbed her coat by the door with Nicole on her heels.

"Why would this arrive in the mail addressed to me?" Nicole offered the envelope to Sam once again. She pushed out her lower lip in a pout. "Please look at it now, before we show your dad."

Sam scowled, took the envelope, and peeked inside.

The smaller, yellowed envelope, a film of dust and age ground into the paper, lay tucked snug at the bottom. Sam couldn't bring herself to reach for the smaller envelope. How long could she stall Nicole? "It's a mystery." Sam stared at the envelope. "But what can I do?"

"Just, read it." Nicole pulled a tissue from her pocket and blew her nose.

Sam stared at the envelope in her hand. This was the point of no return. Once she read it, she was involved whether she wanted in or not, but she owed Nicole, right? After Portland, she owed Nicole two or three.

She read, "*Dear D,*"

Sam raised her gaze to meet Nicole's and raised an eyebrow before continuing in silence to the end. She folded the letter and held it in her hands. "Who is 'G' then?"

"I don't know. I think you might have something in one of your books about it, though."

Sam handed the letter back to Nicole. "What did your mom say?"

"Nothing. I couldn't find her, and I'm freaking out here. But I haven't seen her since before lunch."

"Call her." Sam shrugged.

Nicole glared at her. "Do you think I haven't? Like a million times?"

Sam's fingers tingled as she held the letter. "Okay. Okay. Don't rip my head off. Maybe, she's just at the store." Sam wiped her hands on her jeans. "Something is not kosher with this letter. We'd better get this letter to the throne room for analysis."

Nicole gave a curt nod, and Sam turned away to hide her face. Please let Nicole's mom be grocery shopping.

Chapter Three

The marble steps of the circular staircase were cool to Sam's bare feet as she descended into the throne room. Sweat beaded on her upper lip. Was time travel the only way to address the mysterious letter? Her throat constricted. What did she know about the bricks? Not much.

Nicole followed Sam across the throne room to the huge mahogany table, piles of books on one corner, a cup filled with pens and pencils sitting beside a stack of blank paper. "How's your family doing?" Nicole asked.

"Not good, as you can imagine. Aunt Eli's funeral left us all wacked. I even considered cancelling movie night." She really needed movie night, some popcorn, some laughter. What she didn't need was this letter business.

"But we need your dad and Archie, right? They'll know what to do." Nicole wrung her hands.

Sam froze. "We do need them. I can't do this alone." Sam leaned against Aunt Eli's chair. "Why did this letter arrive now?"

Nicole stiffened. "You don't think—"

Sam covered her eyes. "Don't say his name."

"Stickel—" Nicole clamped a hand over her mouth.

Sam groaned. "I don't know what to think." She tried to push them away, but visions of the Shanghai tunnels ran through her mind.

"We need to focus, Sam. We need a plan, and I might have a theory. Maybe something happened and my great-great-grandma travelled to America from England without ever getting this letter? We need to figure this out." Nicole marched to the vault door. "We have to do something." She spun to glare at Sam.

Sam stood. She hadn't noticed the maroon curtains opened when they'd first arrived. Who had been in the vault and why? This was not a coincidence.

Nicole needed her help, but what should she do? The hair rose on Sam's arm. What if Nicole's mom had disappeared? Was this Portland all over again but for Nicole's family this time?

The Roman bricks stood out from the standard bricks of the vault wall, their longer sides, but shorter fronts made them look like wafers, not bricks, their color a dull orange, not red.

Sam shivered. She could not propel them through time and space again until she'd overcome her fears, and Dad and Mom were exhausted from Aunt Eli's funeral. She was too, but old people needed so much rest.

Aunt Eli's death would delay her training yet again, but when would Dad begin, when she was old herself, like twenty-two? Her stomach tightened. She needed that knowledge now.

If she'd known what touching those bricks would do, the first time, would she have touched them? Yes. The sleepless nights and nightmares were worth it to have Dad back, but she couldn't use them again until she understood the magic behind how they worked. She inhaled to calm her racing pulse.

Nicole shook the letter in her fist. "Come on, Sam. I need help to understand what this letter means, or who knows what will happen?"

"I agree but—" Sam shivered.

"What? You mean, let's wait? No—" Nicole pushed a finger at Sam's chest. "You are going to help me fix this."

"Nicole—"

"I don't want to hear it." Nicole huffed and jammed her hands on her hips, glaring. "This is affecting me now." Nicole's voice wavered. "If you don't think you can do this, I'll go by myself."

Sam stepped back. "How? You can't just use the bricks."

"Why not?" Nicole gawked at her.

Sam shook her head. Had Nicole lost her mind? Did wanting to be safe make her a bad friend? Or should she overcome her fears and help Nicole solve this problem? Sam gulped.

She couldn't use those bricks without understanding their full power. They'd found Grandma Meyers in Portland, and she'd helped them. Who would help them in London? "I have to understand more about how those bricks work before I use them again." She crossed her arms over her chest.

Nicole folded her hands and held them up. "Couldn't we just—"

"Just what? Randomly go back in time? No."

Nicole's face crumpled.

She took Nicole by the shoulders. "Don't touch anything until I get back."

"Wait. Where are you going?" Nicole shook the letter at Sam.

"To get Dad. This might have nothing to do with the bricks." She took a step toward the stairs. "In any case, he needs to know what's going on."

"Wait." Nicole pointed to the vault. "Look. The bricks are glowing. That means something, right? Is it because of this letter and my mom missing?" Nicole spun to Sam, her face ashen.

"Maybe, but Dad will ground me for life if I just use the bricks. Don't do anything until I get back."

Nicole let out a huff of air, her shoulders sagging. "But Mom? She's important, right?"

"Of course." Sam strode to Nicole and stared hard into her eyes. "I'll be right back. Wait for me."

"Bu—" Nicole grabbed for Sam's sweater but got only air. Now what? Did she follow? But Sam was already sprinting up the stairs.

Nicole held up the letter, but the words were fading from the page. She gasped. "Oh no." She stared at the stairs, but Sam was gone. She had to act now. An unfamiliar tug seemed to beckon her, and she let herself fall into the sensation. She turned toward the open vault, the hair on her arms tingling. The bricks glowed with a golden pulse.

She glanced from the vacant stairs to the vault. Then, with her pulse beating in her temples, she reached her hand for the bricks.

****

Sunlight streamed through the second-story windows, illuminating dust motes. In the almost ninety years since Frederick Meyer built the house, you'd think no one had ever dusted. Dad's voice came from his office. He'd closed the door, which meant do not disturb.

Sam rushed across the entry and upstairs. She reached the landing and covered her sneeze. She hesitated at the top of the stairs, but Mom didn't poke her head out of her room. She jogged to the entry below again. Dad's voice mingled with Mom's in the kitchen.

He must have been talking with Mom in his office. Now they were in the kitchen whispering furiously, but about what? She strained to hear, but the last thing she wanted to do was find out it was about her. Maybe it was mom's resentment at having to move, or Dad covering his grief for his favorite aunt.

Nicole was going to go ballistic if she didn't do something to help her with that letter. She sighed as she ambled into the throne room. "Dad's fighting with Mom, so—" Sam skidded to stop. "Nicole?"

She scanned the room and stopped on the yellowed envelope on the floor.

"Nicole?"

She lifted it. The scent of lavender rose from the letter. She glanced around the basement room. The vault doors were open. The bricks were stacked on the floor, the same dull orange, but lavender hung stronger in the air near the vault.

Sam gasped and her stomach lurched. Where was she?

She wouldn't have—

Sam opened the envelope. A different piece of paper floated to the floor. Did Nicole know about this one? Sam unfolded the paper:

S,
I made it. The bricks will transport you here.
Hurry.
N

What the hell? Was she S and Nicole N? Did she just time-travel a note? It looked like it had been written almost one hundred years ago. And how had Nicole used the bricks?

Sam read the envelope again.

Peebles' Pretties Toy Shoppe
44th Market, London

She read the postmark, October 28, 1929, and a flicker of electricity prickled up her arm. She put the note back into the envelope with the letter. If the leap to Portland in 1901 had taught her anything, it was not to trust the bricks. They were dangerous and unpredictable.

Sam scanned the envelope. What was she hoping to find? "London" scrawled in black ink adorned the right corner. 1929. Wasn't that the year the stock market crashed? She typed the address in her maps app. She zoomed out to make sure she was in London.

"Covent Garden? Why?" She glared at the dull bricks.

****

The throne room walls seemed to press in upon Sam as she slouched in the throne. Aunt Eli wasn't here to scold her to respect the furniture or instruct her on her posture, and she was at a loss for what to do.

Would the chair accept her this time? She sank into the cushions and draped both legs over an arm of the ornate chair. She closed her eyes.

A soft thump resonated on the thick wool rug, and then cat feet whispered over the tribal design that had captured her imagination as a five-year-old. Archie.

"Where did you come from?" She scowled at him.

"The vault."

He sat before her in his cat form.

"Did you help Nicole on her travels?"

"I did what my mistress would have told you to do." Archie purred.

Sam sank deeper into the cushions, the bright sunshine a joke juxtaposed against her black mood. "I suppose you did. You loved Aunt Eli, too, so when I say her death stopped time, you get it right? But more than that, she left me with so many unanswered questions, and Dad isn't any help."

Archie just blinked and purred.

"Why didn't Nicole wait for me to help her figure this out? Aunt Eli ran out of time, and Dad won't tell me, and now she's gone." She pressed her fingers to her temples. Maybe if she concentrated, she would hear Aunt Eli's advice too.

"It was important for her to leave when she did, alone." Archie stared at her.

Talking to him in cat form was becoming more and more normal, but was Nicole in danger? Sam rubbed her forehead, as if to wipe those thoughts from her mind. Would this ever make sense?

"Nicole's mother is in trouble." The orange tabby licked his front paw and ran it over his face whiskers.

"I know, I know, but focus, Archie. Nicole went to London, but why Covent Garden, and how will the bricks know to take her to 1929? Are there traces of where she went when she used them, like a magic residue? Isn't that how magic portals work?"

"This knowledge will become clear to you at the proper time." Archie yawned. "But know this, with power comes tremendous responsibility."

She folded her arms over her chest. "But I need to understand that power first, right? Can't you just explain all of this to me?" She spread her arms wide and twirled, indicating all the magical contents in the room.

"Sorry for all the old adages, but here's another one.

Be careful what you wish for." He closed his eyes and tucked his nose under his paws. "It takes time to learn, but as you use the magic, it will become easier."

"You are full of platitudes." She sniffed.

He stretched his front legs out and yawned. "Is that your word of the day?"

"Stupid cat." Sam turned away, unable to stop her grin as his teasing poured from his whiskered mouth. She ran through the events before Nicole's disappearance. She'd raced down the stairs after Nicole, stirring traces of lavender hanging in the air of the throne room.

Was that the scent of the magic?

She scanned the open vault for a glow, but the bricks were not glowing. She would have needed someone with the family blood to transport her, right? Sam ran a hand over the dusty, rough surface of the bricks set into the vault wall. A tug pulled in the center of her chest.

Sam waited for the rush of air from her lungs, but nothing happened. She pulled her hand away.

"Where is she?"

Chapter Four

Sam retraced her steps upstairs. Dad's voice came from his office. Mom must have tired of their fight, or someone called him. She tiptoed to Dad's door and found it ajar. She pushed it open and stared at the leather-bound book lying open on his desk. Sunlight filtered through the blinds and glinted off the key lying on his desk, and there it was—that dreaded aroma of lavender filling the air. She sighed.

Dad glanced at her, covering his phone with one hand. "It's cousin Markus," he mouthed and turned his chair to face the window behind his desk.

Sam hung her head. Aunt Eli's death had hit the whole family harder than she had expected. For Mom, it was the move from their rambler in Magnolia into Aunt Eli's mansion. Sam loved the upper Queen Anne neighborhood, but it was a difficult trek to work for Mom, who complained about arriving at PSU too frazzled to teach her lit classes.

Then there was cool and calm Archie, who was a bundle of emotions. He'd leaned into his reluctance to shift from cat to human form which was understandable. They were all dealing with their grief.

"Thank you, Markus. Talk to you soon." Dad hung up and turned to face Sam. "I know why you're here."

She froze. "You do? This has all gotten so much more complicated."

He grunted. "I know. So much drama. I'm exhausted by all of it, and I hate that you want to rush into this world I don't fully comprehend myself. You're only sixteen for—"

"Dad." She approached the deck and put her hand on his. She loved that he wanted to protect her, but she was sixteen. "Wasn't it Aunt Eli who always said, 'knowledge brings power'? Look, I know Nicole and I could have been killed in Portland because I didn't know how the bricks worked. I still don't." She pulled her hand away. "But now Nicole is in trouble." Her mouth went dry. How was she supposed to tell him the mere thought of using those stupid bricks made her physically ill at the same time she was begging him to teach her about them?

Dad placed his hand on a leather-bound book on his desk before closing it. "Archie filled me in on Nicole's jump through time. She is important, but Archie is monitoring the situation, and he isn't raising the alarm yet. I trust his judgment on the situation, so you will have to focus on one lesson at a time."

"What—" She shook her head. These weren't the words she expected to come out of his mouth. Nicole needed help, and her mom could be in trouble. She bit her tongue.

"Don't rush this. Magic and time-travel takes a toll, and you're so—"

"Young. I know, Dad. Now you sound like Aunt Eli, but what about Nicole's letter?" She pounded on the desk.

"Archie and I are working on that as well as the curriculum for your training, but you must realize, it is five years before I ever wanted you to know about your family obligation. There's no need to rush to grow up.

We still have time."

It was magic. How did he know if they still had time?

Archibald walked into the room. She did a double-take. "Wait. You're not in cat-form."

Dad jumped to his feet. "What's up, Archie?"

Archie cleared his throat. "Your instincts are good, James. It is as you suspected. Someone in the past has activated an artifact, and it may well be the bricks."

"No." Dad rubbed his face. "Was it—"

Sam put a hand to her mouth. "Nicole."

Archie stood at attention, but he was frowning at Dad. "Nicole is involved this time."

She leaned forward in the chair and rested her face in her hands. "No." Sam rose and walked to the window. How did she stop her stomach from churning at the mention of using those stupid bricks? "Dad, I think—"

"Just give me a minute to finish up some business, and I'll join you in the throne room." Dad herded her and Archie out of his office

"What? Dad—"

The door clicked, and she faced Archie.

"He'll help. He must." Archie turned and walked away.

Sam leaned against the wall and slid to the floor, dropping her head onto her knees and clasping her shins. Five breaths and she'd head to the throne room. She closed her eyes.

Nicole was sometime in the past, but how would Sam let her know help was on the way?

Chapter Five

The letter from London weighed on Sam's mind. It lay on the large mahogany table, as any old letter did. Yellowed with age, like so many artifacts and family papers. When Nicole had handed it to her, the familiar tingle ran up her arm to her elbow, which meant magic, right? She had wanted to drop the stupid thing, but didn't.

Her usual comfort at being in the throne room surrounded by Aunt Eli's books did nothing to calm her today. Was she ready for another leap through time? Maybe it wouldn't come to that.

Archie slept on the footstool, and she walked toward the stairs that led up to the entryway. She cupped a hand to her ear. The house was silent except for the usual tics and taps of the central heating system. She climbed the stairs, stopping at step number twelve.

"Twelve represented one's self-importance, emotions, relationships, and pursuit of peace," Aunt Eli had told her.

Sam stared down the curved marble staircase to the throne room. Had Archie been sleeping or spying? Had he heard everything Aunt Eli had taught her? She scoffed, turned, and climbed the steps to the first floor.

Sam sank onto the top step, the closed door to Dad's office meant he didn't want anyone snooping. In the old house, he seldom closed a door and encouraged her curiosity, but after three months in this house, he'd taken to closing his office door.

Archie was doing his best to help her understand the family curse, gift, or whatever, but why was Dad being so secretive? He kept harping on about how young she was. Did he have a mental block?

She pushed herself to a stand. Was that why he let Archie take over? Her stomach tightened, then growled. Hunger affected her ability to concentrate. Maybe all she needed was some lunch because she didn't understand anything any better. Archie was on his fourth lesson, and it was all still Greek to her. She turned to the back of the house and walked in a daze down the Persian carpeted hallway to the kitchen.

The little bit she had learned from Archie had not calmed her fears. She shuddered. It was exhausting hashing over those bricks and this family legacy, the artifacts, time-travel. She didn't trust it, and she couldn't trust Dad. He wasn't telling her everything.

She strolled into the kitchen, her thoughts on artifacts and letters. Dad stood at the sink rinsing tomatoes. He glanced up and gave her a grin before turning back to the tomatoes. "Want a BLT?"

"Sure." She gave him a small smile. She loved him so much.

Should she try again? "Why aren't you helping Archie with my training?"

Dad put the knife down and rinsed his hands. He turned to lean against the counter. "I know you don't trust Archie, Sam, but he's been training guardians since the creation of the bricks. I don't fully understand it myself. Portland was only my second mission, so you know almost as much as I do."

Sam shook her head. "What are you saying? You seemed like you knew what you were doing in the Shanghai Tunnels."

He closed his eyes and sighed.

Why didn't he want to have this conversation? Was he avoiding the throne room? As if that would save him from giving her the answers she needed. Nicole needed her help. "Dad—"

He held up a hand. "I know, and I'll tell you everything, but—"

Archie rushed into the kitchen.

"Now what?" She spun around.

Archie glanced at her, then James. "Sam must resume her lessons in the throne room. We have a lot to cover today."

"Let her eat her sandwich." Dad put the second slice on and cut it into four pieces.

"Time is of the essence." Archie turned and disappeared down the hall.

Sam threw her hands in the air. She did need to eat, but she also needed Archie's instructions. Dad shrugged as he handed her the sandwich on a plate.

"Why is he always so dramatic?" Sam plopped into a chair at the table. She took a bite, but with all the emotions tying her stomach in knots, it tasted like cardboard. She chewed and swallowed anyway.

"Archie is as cryptic as, well, a cat, but if you follow his instructions, you'll have Nicole back before you know it. He hasn't failed this family yet, but there's still a chance you won't have to go. I'll join you both soon." Dad rinsed his hands and disappeared out the kitchen door with a wink to her, balancing his own sandwich on a plate.

What? He wasn't going to eat with her. She pushed the plate away, her hunger forgotten. Dad was stalling. Why won't he help me?

She crossed her arms. "Hmph." Nicole couldn't wait for Archie or Dad to help.

Chapter Six

Nicole pushed wisps of hair from her face and glanced around the dark space. She scowled at the young man holding the lantern. What would Sam do? Act tough? Yes, like she was the one who was angry.

She rose to her feet. "Who cares how I dress, and what's your name?" She stepped into the circle of light. The reflection of the lantern glinted off the inventory-laden shelves: puppet theaters, balls, jump ropes. The rough wood ceiling hung low. Another underground room. Geez.

"Right. You're bossy then. Who do you think you are, the queen herself?" He set the lantern on a crate. "You tell me your name, and I might tell you mine."

She took a step back and held up her hands. Who was she kidding? She wasn't Sam, and she was terrified. "O-o-okay. My name is Nicole Blevins, and I'm not quite sure how I got down here." She shrugged. How much did she tell him without sounding like a lunatic?

"Blevins? Nice to meet you. I'm Wilbert Gordon Smythe."

A shiver ran from her hair roots to her toenails. She took a step back, but he seemed unfazed. She patted the letter in her pocket. Was this the guy? Is that what the "G" stood for?

"Well, that's a start, now, isn't it? Where are you from anyway? America?" His posh accent had the tone of someone in charge, or was it his enunciation that impressed her?

"I am." Nicole waited. She didn't want to offer up too much information.

He cocked his eyebrow. "You realize you're trespassing, and you've terrified the shopkeeper upstairs. He thought he had a ghost in his stockroom." He held the lantern up higher.

She shrank back at his scolding tone. He was waiting for something, but what? She shook her head. What would Sam say? "Sometimes I sleepwalk?"

"A somnambulist?"

"A-what-now?" Nicole cocked her head. "Som-am-bulence?" She bit her lip.

His smooth forehead furrowed. "The Cap' at Bow Street Station sent me to this beat to find the riff raff in the cellar and bring them in. That's you." He frowned at her. "I don't believe you. You're not sleepwalking from anywhere near here, not with that accent, not to mention your clothes." He scratched his head. "So strange for a girl or a boy."

Wilbert had thrown any plan she might have made out the window. Was he going to take her into custody? What could she do?

Nicole heaved a sigh and glared at him. She had to trust someone, and he didn't seem too dangerous, even if he did carry a billy club. He had a lantern.

She held up her hands. "You are right. I lied. I should be in school, but I didn't want to go, so I snuck down here, and you caught me." Her heartbeat quickened. "I need to get to my cousin's house." Really? Her cousin? And who would that be? She placed a hand on her pocket. Maybe that was why she'd received the letter?

Wilbert gave a curt nod. "Finally, something I can believe. Where does your cousin live? I'll escort you there."

He wasn't going to let her go. Nicole dropped her chin to her chest. The letter from London, the Englishman, the bricks had brought her right where she needed to be, but what did she do next?

Chapter Seven

The sharp pine smell of new wood filled the air as Nicole followed Wilbert up the stairs. He held the lantern high enough for her to see. She emerged into a side alley and squinted in the bright light. He led her into a street filled with men all wearing the same flat hats.

She stared at a man who stared back and gestured with a grunt. Wilbert waved his hand toward the man. "Move along. Nothing to see here."

"What was he staring at me for?" She pulled her hood closed and zipped it to her neck.

"Your strange attire, I imagine." He continued his quick pace, weaving through the stacks of boxes and baskets of apples, potatoes, and other produce. He led her around wooden carts pulled by more men in brown, shapeless jackets and women in long skirts and aprons with dark shawls around their shoulders. Some had bonnets tied under their chins. Men wore dirty work clothes, and some wore wool suits with pressed creases. Wilbert's clothes were clean and pressed.

She stood out like a sore thumb in her baggy jeans and pink t-shirt, let alone her chunky platform sneakers. She fell in behind Wilbert, using him as a shield. What should she call him, Wilbert? Mr. Smythe? And what year was it? The clothes weren't from 1901, thank goodness, but they weren't familiar either.

She stood in the alley beside Wilbert. Why wasn't

she freaking out? Was she getting used to time travel? That first rush of air being sucked out her lungs had left her breathless, but that happened every time.

"Where does your cousin live?"

Should she use Darlene as her cousin? She was going to America, but when? Maybe she was still in London. How weird would that be, meeting her great-gran? What would she say to her?

Wilbert cleared his throat. He expected a response.

Mom always told stories of her hilarious great-grandmother, Darlene from London. What was it she'd said? Lincoln Fields. That was it.

"Near Lincoln Fields, I think? Where are we?"

"Why, this is Covent Garden, miss." He turned off the lantern.

Was Lincoln Fields nearby Covent Garden? She had no idea. "I just got here today and got separated from my cousin, so I'm lost." Did he buy her story? He didn't seem alarmed.

"Of course," Wilbert said. "I can see you to Lincoln Fields." He turned and led the way down the alley. "I'm not sure how you got down in that cellar, but it's a short walk to your cousin's."

"Okay." Now what? She didn't know which house was Darlene's. She racked her brain, but there wasn't an address for Darlene on the envelope she'd received. This was a disaster.

****

Sunshine filtered through the stained-glass windows in the throne room, creating colorful patterns on the table. Sam leaned over the *Book of Names,* opened to page 886. She ran her finger down the list. What was it Archie said? She was tracing memory into her brain, that was it.

A tingle ran up her arm when she got to Frederick II and Constance. So weird. She stared at the names, knowing that these people were long gone and buried. She'd met Freddie, though, and that made it weirder.

"Any news?" Dad strolled into the room, a frown wrinkling his brow. He crossed the carpet to stand next to her at the table.

He wasn't going to like what she had to say, but she had to say it anyway. "Dad, there's something I have to tell you."

Dad held out a hand and took hers, leading her to the couch. He guided her down and she sat next to him. "Archie mentioned your fears of the magic. He had to. It stems from not knowing. If you are going to be safe on this trip, I must know everything, especially how you feel, and if you are afraid, we need to conquer that. You were right. Only knowledge will cure that fear."

She leaned against him. It was so like the times he would read to her when she was little.

He wrapped his arm over her shoulder. "When Aunt Eli sent me on my first mission, I was in my thirties and nothing made sense. I thought I could control the magic, but it's not that simple because the magic fits the situation. As the youngest person in our family to time-travel, some fear is natural. As far as I know, no one's leaped at sixteen." He ran his fingers through his hair. "I didn't know anything about the bricks until it was time for me to use them. Baptism by fire, so to speak. It's the uncertainty that upsets your mother, especially now that you are—"

"Time-traveling?"

"Yep. Did you know that Grandma Meyer didn't

find out about the bricks until Bertha arrived in Portland? She threatened to leave her husband if he didn't tell her everything. Stubborn old coot, that Frederick Ludwig Joseph Meyer I." He chuckled. "He would have been your Great-Great-Great-Great—"

"I get it. He was one of the Greats, but he had died before I got to Portland. How did he tell Grandma Meyer?"

"I suppose I could go back and ask him, but it takes me days to recover. It's worse than jetlag." He ruffled her hair.

Sam grinned at him. "Thanks for telling me these things. It's just so weird to be down here without Aunt Eli."

"That woman took her role as Guardian seriously. She was a force to reckon with." Dad chuckled. "So, where are you on the list? Have you found Nicole's branch?"

"I did. Freddie is one of her Greats. Did you know that?"

"I had my suspicions once you two got separated, and she ended up in Seattle." He leaned against the table.

How many times had Sam dreamed of having this kind of conversation with Dad? Finally, he was teaching her and supporting her.

She smiled at him and leaned over the book. "I didn't know Freddie had kids?"

"He moved back to England when he married Constance. Her family lived near Lincoln Park in a beautiful townhouse. Aunt Eli has photos somewhere."

"Did Freddie put some bricks in a tunnel somewhere? Is that where Nicole went?"

"That is the mystery we need to solve, and we might

have to solve it before we rescue her."

Archie rushed into the room, and Dad tensed.

Archie blinked. "Something is wrong."

Chapter Eight

Nicole followed Wilbert down James Street and onto Floral, her lungs aching. Why was it so difficult to breathe? Gym class was failing her, or maybe she should have worked harder because this simple walk was going to kill her.

Wilbert glanced down the stairs. "Do you need help? Your breathing seems erratic."

"My—breathing—is—just—fine." Nicole glanced up and down a sidewalk that seemed to be somewhere in the middle of a row of alleys. Music filtered out of one building, and a woman singing scales out of another. "What is this place?"

"We're in the theater district. Ivor Novello is practicing for *The Vortex?*"

"The Vortex?" She shook her head and shrugged.

"It's a play opening soon at this theater." Wilbert swung his arm to point at the building behind them. He took a step toward her, and she flinched.

How long could she keep up this charade? She needed to take control of this situation somehow. Wait. She could get information, like what year it was. "I'm supposed to get my Nana a paper." She put her hands in her pocket like she'd find a shilling, or a pence, or whatever kind of money they used in England. "I got sidetracked obviously, but—"

"Well, why didn't you just say so?" Wilbert grinned

and led her down Drury Lane and onto a street filled with people.

That worked? She picked up her pace, pressing her hand to her chest. She'd be able to slip away from him as soon as she got the paper. Where would she read it, though? Just get the newspaper, Nicole, and worry about that later.

"Hiya, Mate. Got yesterday's *Gazette*?" Wilbert shook hands with a man by a wooden shack that looked like it would fall over if she sneezed.

She stared at the man. The teeth he had were black, and the spaces where teeth were missing were blacker. His breath almost knocked her down. How could Wilbert stand it? He took the paper handed to him and the man refused Wilbert's offer of coins. Nicole could have wept with relief.

"Today's? Thanks, Barney." He took the paper and saluted.

"Ink's still wet, so …"

Nicole moved to Wilbert's side, and they walked shoulder to shoulder down Drury Lane. "The ink's still wet?"

"He gave me today's edition. Barney's son, Gilly, and I go back to Primary, so—"

Wilbert's voice faded as Nicole glanced at the date on the paper. September 30, 1929. She shuddered and folded her arms over her chest. Was she too late? Had Gran already left for America? She'd never find her house, even if she wanted to.

"—quite a Jack-O-Naps." Wilbert continued and then chuckled.

Nicole chuckled too, hiding the fact that she wasn't listening to a word he was saying. This day just got a lot more complicated.

He took her elbow and steered her through the crowds of men pulling wagons filled with potatoes and squash, women with baked breads and biscuits, and wagons piled with barrels of beer and produce. Her head spun.

"Hello." Wilbert took her arm. "Are you okay, miss?"

His question confused her as blackness closed in.

****

A wave of panic surged through Sam. Archie stood in front of her as she squirmed in Aunt Eli's throne. What if she failed? What if she didn't get the magic? His unblinking eyes bore a hole into her.

"The full process of assimilating knowledge can take as long as nineteen years, depending on the candidate." He jammed his hands on his hips.

She sat on the edge of the chair. "So, what are you saying? The bricks will teach me?"

He brushed the idea from the air with his hand. "No. These things are written in *The Tome of Truth*. Your Aunt made the mistake of not giving the power to your father sooner. When she finally brought your father into the fold, so to speak, he was already in his mid-thirties, ten years later than normal."

Sam closed her eyes. "What does this have to do with anything?"

Archie ignored her. "Then, during his first real mission, you stepped in at fifteen, ten years too soon. It wasn't until we'd all returned home that I realized what the bricks were doing. I'd suspected as much when you were able to use the bricks."

She frowned. "Wait. You knew the bricks were

bypassing Dad?"

"I did." He stood waiting.

She threw up her hands. "Why didn't you say something?"

He blinked. "Say what, exactly? I was sure of nothing. I only suspected."

Sam shook her head and shrugged. "Can you tell me why they call that book *The Tome of Truth* if it changes? Doesn't that change the truth?"

"As I have observed, yes, it does, but I warned your aunt not to wait too long to pull James in. Per usual, she didn't listen." His body shook with the effort to control his breathing. Since when did emotions get the best of Archie? "Losing her daughter had robbed her of the calm logic she needed to train your father. She feared for his life and yours, but then the unimaginable happened."

She threw her hands in the air. "What happened? Nicole used the bricks, but I told her not to touch them, so why did they work?"

He rolled his shoulders as if to relieve stress. "I have my suspicions—"

"But you're not going to tell me, I get it."

Archie stared at her unblinking. "I'm trying to tell you everything you need to know. The bricks dictate so much of who can use them and what activates them."

"Is that why they didn't work sometimes?" Why had she ever touched those bricks, but she couldn't unknow what she knew about them, now. A shudder ran through her, and she pulled her hoodie tighter around her. Archie wasn't giving her answers, but it seemed like he was trying. "What does Dad know? Is it something bad?" She stood and paced the floor.

"He was bound by the bond of truth and loyalty to

the mistress."

"You mean Aunt Eli?"

"Yes." He hung his head.

She wanted to reach out a hand. It was obvious he missed her, and her instinct was to want to comfort. But this was Archie. She crossed her arms over her chest.

He cleared his throat and continued. "She is—was—the Druidess, the Bandrui, sometimes referred to as the Bandorai. The Guardian of the Bricks holds many names."

"I know this, so why—"

Archie held up a hand to stop her questions. "What you need to understand is that the bricks are skipping a generation, and you are the next Guardian. According to the—"

"Wait—" She gulped down a steadying breath. "So, *The Tome of Truth* speaks to you?"

He dropped his chin. "I was there when it was first written, and it has been revised and copied and revised and added to over all the millennia, since Guillem the Wise. But I've had a millennium to study this book and all the artifacts, and I hear every change it makes."

She jumped to her feet and joined him at the table as he ran his fingers over the leather cover. "So, in a nutshell, it's complicated."

Archie nodded. "For the first three hundred years, oral tradition was how knowledge was passed down. In the year 77 BCE, the Guardian, Master Boda, helped capture the knowledge we had on parchment before it was lost forever."

"What do you mean?" Sam held her head in her hands. "You helped write *The Tome of Truth*?"

"Yes, as best I could at that time. We've learned so

much about the magic and the artifacts over the years, such as when the bricks evolve, the truth in *The Tome* changes too."

"So, what you're saying is this isn't an exact science, and the truth changes, and no one knows all there is to know?"

Archie shrugged. "It's an evolving system that responds to people of the blood."

"But how many people have the blood now?" She waited for him to respond. He was holding something back, she could tell. "What is it?"

"You are right about no one truly knowing all there is to know. I've never seen the artifacts work like they do for you. This gift has been—"

She held up her hands and took a step back. "This is a gift?"

He raised a hand. "It may not feel like one, but that's the nature of gifts, and if we are going to help Nicole, you must embrace the knowledge and move beyond your fear. You must trust the power that has come to you from, as you call them, the greats, your ancestors. *The Tome* is the root, the beginning, of your knowledge. The key to *The Tome* must be guarded because the one constant is that another Mr. Stickel will emerge to rupture the time-space-continuum, and we've seen what happens—"

"Names disappear." She plopped on the couch, her head pounding. "So, what you're saying is I can't go back. This is my life now, in French, Gaelic, and Latin?"

He met her gaze and nodded.

Chapter Nine

Boots clattered on a wood floor, and voices echoed down the hall. Nicole pushed her legs over what turned out to be a cot. Had she fallen asleep? Passed out? How had she gotten here?

The walls were white plaster, and the floors were oak. She turned her head. One whole end of the room was a wall of black bars with a door in the middle. Bars? She leapt out of bed and backed into a corner.

This was a jail cell. She put her hand to her mouth to keep from screaming. It was a little too much like the cells in the Shanghai Tunnels. Did Wilbert find out she was lying?

Think, Nicole, think.

She put her hands over her face and inhaled. The fumes of fresh paint filled the air, and she exhaled in a slow hiss. She took her hands away, and Wilbert was standing at the bars holding a cup on a saucer, a quizzical look on his face.

The door isn't locked. Pull yourself together.

"Are you feeling better?" He pushed the door. A loud squeak shattered the silence.

She ran her shaky hands down her pants' legs and stepped from the corner. "Yes. How did I get here?"

"You fainted and hit your head, remember?"

She shook her head. "Not really." She put a hand to her pounding temple. Had it been pounding and his mentioning it made her notice?

"Welcome to Bow Street Station. This was the closest place I could think of to bring you after you fainted." He held out the cup, which sloshed with tea.

She took it and sipped. It was hot but refreshing. She took another sip and sank onto the cot, glancing at the newspaper lying next to her. She'd have to read that when she got a chance.

"So, you work here?"

"I'm a Bow Street Runner, yes." He tugged on his coat and pulled his shoulders back.

She took another sip of the tea. He'd put cream and sugar in it, and it was rejuvenating. "Thanks for the tea." The floral aroma calmed her.

"Everyone gets a cuppa, even prisoners, not that you are a prisoner." He smiled then turned to leave.

"Wait. You're leaving? How long do I have to stay here?"

"I'm just going to check in with the Sarge. When you can walk without fainting, I can take you to your cousin's." He paused as if waiting for permission to leave.

She ran her hand over her hair. Why did she care how she looked? She was in 1929 London, but what was she supposed to do when Darlene might have already left for America? She took a big gulp of tea. This was way too complicated. Where was Sam?

"That's right. Drink it down and you'll feel right as rain in no time."

Bells clattered and she jumped. The racket filled the whole building, and Wilbert poked his head out of the cell. A man barked orders from the front desk.

Wilbert turned to her, his frown casting a shadow

over his eyes. "We have an emergency call. I must go, but the door is unlocked. Can you wait for my return?" He didn't wait for her to respond but disappeared down the hall.

The bells ceased, and silence crackled through the air. She drank the last of the tea and set the cup and saucer on the cot. She tucked the paper under her arm, stood, and strode down the hall, and out the door.

****

The road in front of the Bow Street Station curved out of sight in both directions. It was quieter in this neighborhood than in Covent Garden. Nicole glanced left, then right. Which way had Wilbert led her? She heard merchants calling out their wares: fresh bread, pork pasties, and potato wedges. Nicole's stomach rumbled.

She followed the pull in her gut. Her feet led her down Bow Street to Floral, where she turned right. She stopped, but the urge to walk on pulled her forward. Was this part of the bricks' magic or the letter she'd received, or both? She took a step, which became two and then three. She turned right onto James Street and stopped in front of a toy shop. Wasn't this where she'd landed? A metal door on the side of the building drew her attention. A padlock hung open on a latch.

She pulled the door open with a screech and stepped into the dim stairwell. She closed the door behind her and let her eyes adjust. Of course, this is where the magic would lead her, back to the bricks.

****

Sam looked up from the list of names in the book before her as Archie walked into the room. Her finger rested on Nicole's family tree, the names fading. The tingle that ran up her arm became a jolt that made her jump. "I felt—what was that?"

"That's what I came to tell you." Archie rubbed his hands together.

Sam's mouth went dry.

"It's Nicole." He put his hand on Sam's arm. "Things have changed. You need to go to 1929 London now."

"And do what?" Sam glared at Archie. "I'm not ready." Would she ever be ready? Sam's stomach tightened.

Archie stood before her, his amber eyes unblinking. "The letter is fading."

"The whole letter?" Sam's throat tightened. *Nicole?*

Archie stared at the floor. "The ink is disappearing."

"Like the disappearing names on the family tree?" Sam glanced down at the page. Some of the names were gone. "No. Nicole." Her heart hammered in her chest.

Dad entered the room and joined her and Archie at the table. "Dad, look."

Dad stared at the page, then at Archie. "If she has to go, I'm going with her, but we better have a solid plan this time."

"I'll do my best, but Stickel is up to no good, and Nicole's very existence is in danger." Archie's large yellow eyes did not blink. "We must move quickly."

The hair rose on the back of Sam's neck. "Okay." Her voice was shaky. Nicole needed her. She backed away from the table. "How can I help Nicole, if I don't under—"

"You must take this letter with you."

Sam gawked at Archie. "How will that help?"

"So, it's come to using artifacts already?" Dad

raised his eyebrows. "I understand."

Archie held up a deep purple velvet purse with a silk ribbon pull string handle. He put the letter in it and handed it to Sam. "This will take you to Nicole. Together, you will have to solve this mystery."

She took a step back, but Dad put a hand on her shoulder.

"You wanted to know everything about the bricks and time-travel? I don't even know everything, and neither does Archie because the rules are constantly changing. The best we can do is monitor the books and the artifacts in the vault, so they aren't used for selfish gain."

"How many are there?" Had she said that out loud? She put a hand to her lips. Her mind reeled with all this information at once.

"Several. The number changes with each mission. I'm sorry, Sam, but magic isn't an exact science, and time changes our understanding of the world as we know it."

"That doesn't help, and I still don't know enough. I'm not ready." A tightness gripped her stomach, and she wrapped her arms around her chest. "Nicole," she whispered.

Dad squeezed her shoulder. "You know enough, and you will be there to help Nicole. I wish I could give you more specific instructions, but that's how it works sometimes."

She growled under her breath and glanced from Dad to Archie, who gave a weak smile more like a grimace.

Archie put his hand on her shoulder and stared unblinking into her eyes. "Someone will be monitoring the books and the artifacts on this end, and I'll do what I can to make this a better trip."

"That does help a little, but I'm still—"

"I hate to say this, but look." Archie held up the book. "The ink is fading faster than the hands on the clock are ticking."

"Okay. I'll do it for Nicole." She glanced at the bricks.

"Ready?" Archie pointed to the purple satchel that held the letter. "Don't lose it."

She accepted the purple velvet purse from Archie and walked to the bricks. She held out her hand, then pulled back.

****

The pressure on her chest pushed out all the air in her lungs. She landed with a thump, and the rumbling of a vehicle approaching startled her. A tang like the motor oil that clung to Grandpa's work overalls filled the air, and she spun around.

"What the heck?" She jumped back as a small train rumbled past her down the track. She stood in a round tunnel with tracks running down the center and dim lights located every ten feet or so in the ceiling.

Was this where she was supposed to be? She turned in a circle, patting her shirt for the purse. It was gone.

Her eyes adjusted to the dark, and a lump of purple lay beside the tracks where she'd landed. "Thank heavens."

Was this London? What year was it? She bent at the waist and counted to six each time she inhaled, held her breath as she exhaled, and held her breath, then started over. Of all the things Archie had taught her, this was the most useful so far.

Why did magic have to be so stressful? She focused

on her pulse that slowed with each breath. Nicole must have landed near here, right, but that was days ago. Would the same amount of time have elapsed in this time? Why hadn't she thought to ask Archie about those configurations during their lessons?

"Nicole?" She cupped a hand by her ear and turned around in the tunnel. "Nicole?"

****

The darkness in the tunnel was broken by single bulbs hanging from the rounded ceiling and casting shadows. Sam wiggled her toes and her fingers. They still worked, but her legs wobbled. Would she be able to stand?

Someone opened a door, and slow steps proceeded down into the tunnel from a ladder bolted to the wall. Was it Nicole? Dust hung in the air, and she wiped at her nose to stop the itch. She tucked her head in a crouch. Was this how she found Nicole, hiding behind a barrel? Whoever was coming down the stairs would find her in about ten seconds, so how did she want to be found? She peeked from her hiding spot as a girl in Nicole's jeans and Doc Marten boots scanned the tunnel in both directions.

Sam stepped from her hiding spot. "Nicole," she hissed.

"Who's there?" Nicole's round eyes and disheveled hair changed her appearance, but it was Nicole.

Sam stood and took a step.

"Sam? Is it really you?" Nicole rushed to her and wrapped her arms around her.

Sam pulled her friend in tight. Archie said that Nicole would help, and somehow, she had. Did the bricks know to land her in the same place? "How did you find me?"

"What? How did you find me?" Nicole chuckled. "I landed in a stockroom just up there." She pointed to a yellow glow in the wall. "Wait. Are the bricks still active?"

"They are super dim, so they are probably phasing out."

"Right. That makes sense. We just got here, and we probably have to do something. I mean, why else would we be here?"

Sam nodded and put a hand on Nicole's shoulder. "Finish your story."

Nicole rubbed her hands on her jeans. "Well, apparently someone from the toy shop heard me in the stockroom and called the cops, and a police officer came and took me to Bow Street Police Station, and—"

"What? Slow down." Sam hugged Nicole tighter then released her. "Okay. Now, why were you taken by the police? Are you okay?" Sam held Nicole at arm's length in front of her. "What horrible luck. This is shaping up to be a Portland redux, isn't it?" That was the last thing Sam needed right now. Why did time travel have to be so terrifying?

"I was so frightened, but, the policeman, Wilbert, was understanding and helpful. I can't believe you're here." Nicole's voice was low but still echoed.

"Wilbert? So, you're on a first-name basis with the police?" Sam stared at her friend, then hugged her again. "I don't care. I'm so relieved I found you. Now we can look for Darlene."

"Why?"

"Because the names on your family tree are disappearing, and the letter appeared addressed to you, and because Archie said." A sense of purpose filled Sam, and she focused on her friend. "You're right. We have work to do before we can go home."

Nicole's shoulders sagged. "Of course, we do. There's always something, right? What is it this time? Another murder? Another bank robbery where no money was stolen?"

Sam shrugged. "I'm not sure what it is we'll have to do specifically, but I do know that—"

"We have to do something to save the names from my family disappearing." Nicole pulled the paper from inside her jacket. "This might help." She slapped the paper against her hand. "Wilbert got it from Barney, today's paper. Guess the date."

Sam shrugged. "Just tell me." She meant it. Being in this storeroom made her vulnerable. "We'd better find a place where we can read it from cover to cover. Maybe it holds the clue to finding Graham."

"But what about the date?" Nicole scowled. "Aren't you even curious?"

Sam swallowed then cleared her tight throat. "Fine. What day is it?"

"September 30, the same day I received the stupid letter in our time, except it's 1929."

Chapter Ten

One set of footsteps echoed down the tunnel, and a shiver ran down Nicole's arms. She clutched Sam and backed behind a metal locker bolted to the wall. She held up a finger, and Sam nodded.

"Who's down here?" It was a man's voice.

Sam clamped her eyes shut. "I hope that's your policeman." She shrank farther into the corner.

"It sounds like Wilbert." Nicole stood and walked into the tunnel, avoiding the tracks.

Wilbert called out. "Miss Blevins? I thought I told you to wait for me at Bow Street Station? How did you get down here again?" He frowned.

"Sorry." Nicole grimaced. "It's a long story."

Sam stood and joined Nicole.

Wilbert raised his billy club and pointed it at Nicole. "Wait. You brought a friend? What's going on here?" He ran his gaze up and down Sam, taking in her boots, her jeans, and her hoodie. "Why are you dressed like that?"

Nicole stepped between Wilbert and Sam and pressed her shoulders back. "Let me explain, Officer Smythe. This is my fault."

"Officer?" Wilbert scratched his head. "I'm not in the military."

"Officer?" Sam took a step back.

Nicole put her hands up. "Right. This is the guy I met. He took me to jail."

Sam glared at Wilbert.

"Sam." Nicole put a hand on Sam's shoulder, but she shook it off.

"Now listen." Wilbert held up both hands and shook his head. "I only took her there because she fainted." He glanced at Nicole. "You look fine now, miss, but I might have to take you to Bow Street Station for breaking the law. Twice. I told you—"

"To wait for you. I remember." Nicole smiled. "I had to find my other cousin, though. We're both from—"

He held up his hand. "No more lies, you cheeky American devil."

"I'm not lying." Nicole crossed her fingers behind her back. "This is my cousin, Sam, and I had to meet her in Covent Garden, but we got lost looking for a tea shop. We wanted to buy my aunt a gift of tea. Can you recommend a shop?" Nicole glanced over her shoulder at Sam, who was squirming and shaking her head. Now what?

"I might know of a place, but you have to promise me that you won't return to the tunnels as soon as I'm gone." He jabbed the billy club in their direction again.

Nicole clutched Sam's arm tighter and stood her ground. Having Sam by her side gave her strength? She blinked. Cousins. She wished she was related to her best friend.

Nicole nodded. "You are a lifesaver. We will follow you."

Wilbert tipped his hat and turned. "Lifesaver?" he mumbled and led them to an exit.

"This is the way I came. It was like my instinct was leading me to you," Nicole whispered in Sam's ear.

"I can't believe you found me. Did you ask him about the letter?" Sam clutched Nicole's hand as they crossed the tracks following Wilbert.

"How? He's already suspicious of me. The letter was to Darlene from 'G,' and this guy is G." Nicole tipped her head to one side.

Sam opened her mouth to respond, but Wilbert cut in.

"My name is Wilbert at work, but my friends call me by my middle name, Gordon."

"Oh." Sam stared at Wilbert. Was this G? Could they have found the author of the letter?

He stopped and raised the lantern. "Did you think I couldn't hear you whispering?"

"Wha—" A stabbing pain shot through Sam's head, and she doubled over pressing her fingers to her temples.

"Are you okay?" Wilbert closed the space between them and held up the lantern.

Sam forced herself to stand up straight. What was going on right now? Was this supposed to happen?

"Wait. Did you say Darlene? Is your cousin Miss Darlene Meyer?" Wilbert let the lantern droop as he lost focus.

His voice had quavered when he said her name. What did that mean? Was he the letter writer? Is he why the names were disappearing?

Chapter Eleven

The Covent Garden chaos echoed off the wooden
walls of flower shops and laundries. Wilbert marched
down the cobbled street, slapping the billy club in his
open palm. Was he angry? Sam matched his quick pace.

She linked arms with Nicole. Perhaps Wilbert was
nervous? She cleared her throat, and he turned to her.
"Are you going to hit someone with that thing? Doesn't
that hurt your hand?"

Wilbert stopped and shook his head as he turned to
face them, his lips pressed together in a thin line. "Not at
all. I'm trying to figure out how Nicole ended up in the
toyshop stockroom, and then with you in the Royal Mail
rail tunnel. Something isn't clear with your story, and I
hate being lied to." He jabbed a finger at Nicole, "Plus I
specifically told you—"

Sam stepped in front of Nicole. "It's my fault. I was
supposed to meet her on the corner of Drury Lane and
Floral Street, but I got lost. She searched and finally
found me in the tunnel, then you showed up."

"Right." Wilbert planted his hands on his hips and
glowered at them. "That story stinks to high heaven." He
shook his head. "So, did you say you two are related?"

"Yes." Sam nodded her head. Did this mean he
believed them, or would at least pretend to believe them?
Is this how time travel usually worked? Lying until
people just gave in and helped you?

"No," Nicole said, then slapped a hand over her mouth.

Sam shook her head at Nicole. "You're not helping."

Wilbert scratched his head. "So, which is it because I'm confused." He waited, but Sam didn't know what to say.

"One thing is becoming very clear to me. You two haven't spoken one word of truth since I met you. You don't accidentally end up in a stockroom or in the mail rail tunnel by accident. Are you in trouble of some sort?" He crossed his arms over his chest and planted his feet shoulder-width apart. "Are all Americans as confused as you two?"

Sam was fresh out of lies, so what was she supposed to do now? Go with the confused American idea? She inhaled and counted to six before speaking. "Listen Wilbert, I know how this looks, but we are lost, and when Nicole disappeared, I wandered—"

"Stop. I don't want to hear any more. I believe you are lost, but the rest is all lies. If you're in trouble, I can help. It's my job, but if you can't be honest with me—"

Honesty. What a novel concept. Was this what Archie and Dad had been doing the entire time, being honest but withholding the truth? Time travel really was too much for the average brain to comprehend.

She leaned to Nicole. "Should I tell him the truth?"

Nicole put a finger to her lips and shook her head. Even she didn't want to end up in the insane asylum.

"Can't you just show us where Lincoln Fields is. We can find Darlene and—" She glanced over her shoulder at Sam and opened her mouth, but nothing came out.

Bells began to chime in the distance. She counted

three rings. They set a pleasant, old-world, fairytale tone, and she took in the quaint tea shops and fabric shops alongside run-down spice and vegetable shops in need of paint and a good scrub. The scent of fresh baked cookies blended with a rotten fish carcass aroma filled the air. How had she not noticed that before?

She shifted from foot to foot. "Listen, Wilbert—"

"Before you say one more thing, I want you to know I'm on your side." He pulled his hat off his head and gripped the rim. "You're not going to survive the night on the street in Covent Garden, and if there isn't a cousin for you to go to, I need to know right now. It will be dark by 6:00, and you need to be safe inside someplace." He glanced at Nicole. "I guess you could stay at the Bow Street Station in a cell, unless we're full."

"A cell might be okay until we can find Darlene." Nicole took her hand from Sam's and crossed her fingers behind her back.

His forehead relaxed as he smiled. It transformed his face. Sam ran her hand over her hair, but stopped. Was she primping for this guy?

He hung his billy club on his belt before turning on his heel and walking down a side road. She took Nicole's hand back into hers and fell in step behind him. When should she tell Nicole they were cousins for real? Maybe after they found Darlene's house and sent Wilbert back to Bow Street?

****

Archie pulled out the collar of his shirt and scratched the back of his neck. How did humans wear these itchy clothes anyway? The clatter of footsteps on the stairs startled him. He looked up from the Bible as James burst into the basement, wiping his sweaty forehead on his sleeve. James carried *The Tome of Truth*. Archie stared at it. The lock held the key with matching lavender cord. There was only one reason James would carry it from the library.

Archie put up a hand to stop James as he approached the table and lifted the map. "Wait—"

James ignored him and perused the streets of Covent Market. "I may not be the next Guardian, Sam is, and it was only a matter of time before Sam takes charge in her own way, but I can still help, can't I?"

James placed the book at one end of the table and pulled the map over to him. He ran his hand over the old paper, his eyes scanning the roads and bridges. "Can you pinpoint their location?" James never looked away from the map. He stabbed his pointer finger into the map. "Point it out."

"I can't locate their exact position, but I can sense that they are in Covent Garden, and I'm fairly certain they are near this toyshop, but—"

"I don't want to hear any 'buts' from you. This is Sam's life on the line." James glowered at Archie.

Archie straightened his spine and turned to face James. If James couldn't control his emotions, Sam might never be found. "Calm heads must prevail."

"Don't give me that, you stupid cat." James clenched his fists and pressed them against his temples. "I'm sorry. It's just—"

"She's your child, and Nicole is her best friend. I do understand, but no."

Archie would hate using the *Glemme* potion again. After Bertha's disappearance, he'd had no choice but to dose Mistress Elise. She'd forgotten almost everything, but when she finally remembered enough to put the pieces of Bertha's disappearance back together, she'd fostered a mistrust of his abilities and became hyper-vigilant and look where that left James.

He'd dose James with *Glemme* as a last resort. It had taken five years for the mistress to forgive him for dosing her. Archie cleared his throat. He respected James, but his parental love was standing in the way. It was too powerful and unpredictable.

"What do you mean, no? I was searching through *The Tome of Truth*." He lifted the velvet book. "Look at this passage."

Archie glanced over James' shoulder and stepped back. The words on the page were jumbled. "That's not right. When did this happen?"

"Has this happened before? Think, Archie. Before it's too late for Sam and Nicole." James brushed his hair from his eyes.

"I will do what I can. Leave the book with me, and I'll try to decipher what this means. All I know is they are together." *And they may be running out of time.* But he didn't speak those last words.

James threw his hands in the air. "I must go back. They need help."

"No, James. If Portland taught us anything—"

"It's because of Portland I need to go. Sam was almost Shanghaied. Stickel was desperate and dangerous. We have to stop him before—" James pounded the table.

Archie took a step back. It wasn't a matter of if, but when he was going to have to brew the potion.

Chapter Twelve

The aroma of lavender and the sharp scent of bleach clung to Sam's clothes, a byproduct of her jump through time. She rubbed her nose and followed Nicole as Wilbert led them down Floral in a light drizzle. For October, the London day was warm but overcast, a lot like Seattle. A bang filled the air, and Sam jumped. She gripped Nicole's arm.

"Was that a gun?" Nicole stopped.

Wilbert stopped, his head tilted. "Gun? Who would have a gun? It was someone's old jalopy backfiring."

"Jalopy?" Sam hesitated. The wooden shops and buildings on this street needed a coat of paint, and vegetables rotted at the side of the road. "I don't know what a jalopy is, and why didn't anyone else react?"

Wilbert cocked a hip and rubbed his chin with the fingers of his right hand. "Hmm. A jalopy is a car, and sometimes the older ones create a loud bang. It's a fuel to oxygen ratio problem." Wilbert kept walking through the crowds as if nothing had happened. "Doesn't that happen in America?"

He wove through working men with loose jackets and berets. Was that their working uniform? Some wore white aprons, some pushed wheelbarrows filled with apples or potatoes, and some pulled carts with squeaky wheels. Women walked arm and arm, chattering nonstop in a language that didn't resemble English, but Sam suspected probably was. An old black car drove through the crowds and backfired, supporting Wilbert's claim. A horse reared, and Sam cowered with Nicole against a brick building.

Wilbert stopped and glanced over his shoulder. He turned and placed a hand on Nicole's arm. "Are you okay, miss? Did the automobile scare you?"

Sam chuckled. "You are kind of pale. Do you feel all right?"

Nicole ignored her. "We aren't used to ca— automobiles backfiring, so a bit frightened, yes."

Was she batting her lashes? He was good-looking, but what was going on? Nicole couldn't fall for Wilbert. He was—

"We're almost to the station. I'd like to have Graham, my fellow bobby, join us." He turned and strode away, Nicole's head turning as he moved.

Sam tugged on Nicole's sleeve. "Graham? Could Graham be 'G?' And are you checking him out right now? Really?"

Nicole shrugged her hand away. She glowered at Sam. "No, I'm not, and Graham could be 'G.' This is getting complicated."

"We need to stay focused."

Nicole tried again to shrug free of Sam's hand.

"You think he's cute?" Sam stared at Nicole.

Nicole squirmed. "Yeah, so what? We're going back to the future soon, right?"

"Nicole, I have to tell you something else, and you're not going to like it." Sam inhaled a shaky breath.

"Really? I just think he's cute. Why all the drama?" Nicole waited, her brow furrowed.

Sam exhaled and blurted. "Archie found your family

tree in the Big Bible. It's why you could use the bricks when we were in Portland."

"What?"

"You have the blood."

Nicole shook her head. "The blood? Like—" She pointed to her wrist.

Sam nodded. "Apparently, and we're related."

Nicole's eyes went blank as she stared into space. Was she going to freak out now? Nicole turned and sneezed into her elbow. She wiped her nose on her sleeve. "What did you say?"

"Freddie is one of your Greats, and Wilbert might be—"

"Eww!" Nicole backed away from Sam, her stomach tying into a knot. "You mean—"

"Yes. You can't crush on one of your Greats."

"Oh my—" Nicole bent at the waist.

Sam forced the grin from blooming on her lips. "It's okay. It's clear he cares about you, about us both, but Wilbert loves Darlene, who is your other Great."

"Wait a minute. So that means that I was pretending that Darlene was my cousin, but she really is a relative?" Nicole leaned against the wall for support as she let a breath release in a whistle. "This changes everything."

"Kind of, right?"

"That means we're distant cousins?"

Sam nodded and grinned. "You're my best friend and my cousin, and you can use the bricks. How great is that?"

Nicole stared at Sam. "Is it great though? Look where we are, right? And we need to solve another mystery, and it's probably yet another problem created by—" Nicole ground her teeth.

"Stickel. Agreed." Sam waited a beat before adding. "Who is also related to you, by the way."

"Don't remind me!" Nicole put her hands to her face. "How did I not know this before I touched those stupid bricks? It does explain why I could use the bricks. I still have nightmares about that, you know."

Sam nodded in agreement. If Nicole could get through this shock without a blowup, it was a win-win for this mission. "Archie has been going over the magic and *The Tome of Truth*. I still have a long way to go, but it's a start."

Nicole scratched her chin. "I guess I'll be joining you at the School of Archie." She shook her head. "This is too weird, and I'm so embarrassed about Wilbert."

Sam nudged Nicole's shoulder. "Don't worry about it. He's more concerned about Darlene. I don't think he even noticed you making googly-eyes at him. Besides, it's probably your relationship with Darlene that makes him so protective of you right now."

Nicole rolled her eyes. "So, we wait for one of my Greats to help us solve this Stickel-snafu?"

"That's a plan." Sam watched Wilbert's broad shoulders as he strode down the cobbled road. "He's a good man."

Nicole bobbed her head. "You're right. Gran's name is Darlene." Nicole's focus never left Wilbert, and she jogged to catch up with him.

Sam stopped. "I remember that name." Her finger pulsed with the memory of running her finger over the list in the genealogy book. Darlene was Grandma Meyer's name, but it was also Nicole's great-great-grandmother, but it was Darlene's husband's name that was disappearing.

Chapter Thirteen

Sam fell into step behind Wilbert. The street they were on curved, and she read Bow Street on the sign. She glanced down the road that did, in fact, bow, and glanced at Nicole, who shrugged.

"If I'd paid attention the first time." She put a hand to her head. "But I passed out."

"Why?"

"I don't know. I went woozy, then that was it." Nicole glanced at Wilbert, her cheeks blooming a rosy glow. "He must have carried me to the Bow Street Station. I woke up on a cot here. He didn't have to do that." She placed a hand over her heart.

Sam opened her mouth to say something, but Wilbert stopped in front of a building. Another bobby emerged, adjusting his hat over his red curls.

Wilbert waved him over. "Graham. I say, Graham."

Graham raised his hand and jogged down the steps, striding toward them. "Wilbert." He clasped Wilbert's hand, and they shook.

Nicole traded a glance with Wilbert, and a small grin formed on her lips. Was she melting?

Sam nudged her. "What are you doing?"

"Shhh." Color rose to Nicole's cheeks. Since when was Nicole interested in some random guy in the past? Oh, right, Portland, but then, they'd all crushed on someone.

"I'd like to introduce you to Nicole and Sam. They're from America."

Graham glowered at them. "America?" He paused, then opened his mouth to say something.

Wilbert interrupted. "Nicole knows Darlene."

Oh no. What had they done? Would Graham know who Darlene knew? Sam tensed.

"Distant cousins." Sam stuck her hand out to shake, but Graham didn't take it. She dropped her arm to her side. "From America. She probably won't recognize us."

Nicole stepped up to join Sam. "That's right. We made the trip without writing to her first. We didn't realize it would be so difficult to find her on our own."

Graham crossed his arms. Sam grimaced. He was a little bit too much like a policeman. "Are you from the docks then? Is that where your trunks are?"

Sam shuffled her feet and nodded. "Um. Yes?" That didn't sound very convincing.

Nicole bobbed her head in agreement. "That's right." She put a hand on Sam's arm. "Remember, Sam? The conductor gave us a baggage ticket."

"You mean the steward, right?"

"Graham, where are your manners? These girls have had a long voyage and haven't had tea."

Graham scoffed. "I don't believe these girls, and I don't care how different their clothes, or how fine their boots. Why are they dressed as boys? This is very suspicious." He tapped his toe on the pavement.

"Are you going to help or not? They need to find Darlene, and I'd like to do that before I'm off duty."

Sam closed her eyes. Wilbert didn't have to help, but he was, and she crossed her fingers behind her back that he'd continue to do so, even if he had only just met them.

Graham huffed, scowling at Wilbert, then Nicole, to her. Was Graham being protective of Darlene? She admired that, but if he stood between Nicole meeting her Great, what would they do? She leaned into Nicole who put a hand over hers.

"Listen, Graham. Our voyage was long, and we're exhausted." She cleared her throat and continued. "If you could please help us find Darlene's house, we'll do the rest. She'll recognize Nicole."

Nicole's body went stiff, and Sam winced. She knew better than to lie without first warning Nicole. Sam's stomach tied into a knot.

Wilbert pulled Graham aside. What was he saying?

Sam whispered in Nicole's ear, "I know your family tree, and we can use Grandma Meyer and Elise to convince your Great-Great." She squeezed Nicole's hand. "Please, follow my lead. Trust me."

"Okay. That should work. You are related, and we've met Grandma Meyer. If Darlene has too, she'll know we aren't lying." Nicole's shoulders relaxed.

Graham stood with his arms still crossed. Wilbert smiled at her, and she held his gaze. What beautiful hazel eyes.

Sam nudged her.

"Right." Nicole took a step forward. "I'm Nicole and this is Sam. We'd really appre—"

"So, you know Darlene, do ya?" Graham shook his head. "I have a call to make. I am on duty, you know. Then, if I have time."

"I'm still on duty myself." Wilbert followed Graham into the station.

"Do you think they believe us?" Nicole wiped her hands on her jeans.

Sam shrugged. How long would Graham leave them waiting on the sidewalk? She bit her nail, and Nicole swatted her hand away. "Ow." She nudged Nicole.

Graham placed his hat on his head as he came out of the station and jogged down the steps, Wilbert following close behind. "Her house is on the way to my first call, a peeping Tom." He scowled. "And you lot have made me late. Keep up now." He strode away.

The old wooden buildings and rank odors of rotting vegetables and fruit gave way to sidewalks and trees lining the street. Nannies pushed prams with babies sleeping inside. Sam collided with Graham's broad back as he stopped on the sidewalk.

Why was he staring at Nicole? She blushed and put a hand to her cheek. What did he see? She stared back at him.

A grin broke out on his face, and he nodded at Nicole. "It took me a while, but it hit me just now. I see your resemblance to Darlene."

Nicole gave him a wide-eyed stare and a small smile. "I said I was." Graham looked away as if embarrassed.

"Right then. To Darlene's."

Sam took Nicole's arm. "I'm so glad he came around."

Had Graham's name been part of the family tree? But it had faded, so how was finding him supposed to work? Didn't Archie say the answer was supposed to present itself? But it didn't. Why did this have to be so difficult?

"Why are you staring at him?" Nicole leaned close.

Sam glanced at her, then back at Graham and Wilbert. Everyone was waiting for her to say something.

"Sorry. I didn't realize. I mean—"

Wilbert cleared his throat and patted Sam on the shoulder. "We should find your cousin's house, right?"

Sam ventured a smile. "Yes."

Graham and Wilbert resumed their march down Great Queen Street.

Nicole pulled Sam close and hissed in her ear. "That was a close one. Wilbert seems to be on our side, but does he suspect we're still lying?"

"I hope not. Let's just follow his lead." She nodded at Nicole. "Our best plan is to find Darlene."

"And I have to get to my call." Graham turned.

"Graham, quit lying. I know this isn't a peeping Tom case. What are you up to?" Wilbert cocked an eyebrow.

"If you must know, I want to tell her something in person." Graham bustled down the street.

Wilbert pressed his lips together, and his face lost all color.

Sam pulled Nicole behind her. Her gut twisted, and she had learned to trust her gut. Wilbert was reacting to something, but what?

****

Spring sunshine brightened the throne room as James leaned both arms on the table and hung his head. He inhaled. Archie was such an obstacle sometimes, but why now?

"What do you mean I can't go?" James searched Archie's face. "She's my daughter's best friend, and names are disappearing. Again. What's happening?"

Archie adjusted the vest of his wool suit and pushed his shoulders back. "I do not know, but if you would give me a moment."

71

James threw his hands in the air. "Please enlighten me."

"It's tied to the letter, the disappearing names, and the fact that Sam and Nicole have not found Darlene yet. She must soon if she is going to correct the problem created by Stickel before Darlene leaves London for America, and my guess is they have seventy-two hours at the most." Archie made a slight bow as though he was addressing royalty. Archie followed all the old protocol as when he discussed missions with Aunt Eli, everything that is but to call him "Sir," which he knew James despised.

"That's only three days." James raked his hand through his short, graying hair. "Sam, you're on restriction for life after this leap."

"It will be enough time. Since the bricks have chosen Sam—"

"I must go." James clenched his teeth. Archie was right. This magic had rules, but if he helped, it wouldn't interfere and disrupt the transfer of the Guardianship, would it?

Archie stared at James. Could he see the wheels turning in his mind? See that he was connecting the dots?

"You need to let Nicole and Sam work this out. It is the only way to resolve the issue of the names and save Nicole."

"But a new name is appearing in the Bible where the old one disappeared, and we have no idea how that name will change the present, if at all?"

Archie stared at James. This clinched it. The *Glemme* potion was the only way to calm the poor man.

Chapter Fourteen

James took the stairs two at a time and stopped on the star in the middle of the entry. How would he explain to Carol that the bricks were active again? She barely kept her sanity when Aunt Eli tried to explain the bricks the first time, especially after she found out Sam had used them. He didn't have a fraction of Aunt Eli's knowledge, so where did he begin this time? He paused.

Maybe he didn't have to tell her? But she was his wife. He had to tell her, right?

"Carol?" He winced as his voice echoed off the two-story vaulted entry ceiling. It allowed sound to travel to all the bedrooms. He inhaled, then jogged up the spiral stairs to the second floor. The windows from the sunporch filled the landing as he crossed to their bedroom suite and opened the door. "Carol."

Carol strolled out of the walk-in closet a frown on her face. "James, you startled me. Must you barge in like a water buffalo?"

A chill filled his core, and he took her hands. Where did he begin, with the letter, Nicole's disappearance, Sam's need to help her?

He pulled her into his arms. "You are such a good mother. I can't believe—"

She pushed him away. "Don't give me the good mother speech. What's up?" She stabbed a finger at his chest. "This has to do with the bricks, doesn't it? I can't do this right now. It's too soon." Carol clamped her eyes shut. "I don't care what Aunt Eli said. Sam is too young."

James pressed his lips together. If he spoke now, he could anger her. His heart pounded in his chest as he rolled his shoulders to relieve the tension. There was no turning back now. "She is too young. I agree, but Nicole has set the bricks in motion again."

"Nicole? How, and what year did they jump to this time? How am I supposed to be okay with this?" She threw her hands in the air.

"It's hard—"

"Ya think?" She paced the floor in front of the mirrored closet doors, her petite figure tense and graceful, like a jaguar poised to pounce. She was a fierce mother.

God, he loved this woman in all her five foot four glory.

She flared her nostrils. "Don't you dare look at me like that." She shook her forefinger at him. "I can't wrap my head around it, let alone my heart. Not when I see our daughter suffer like this. You have left too much to chance with this magic. I need more assurance for Sam's safety."

James stared into his wife's eyes. Was he going to lose her over this family magic? How could he de-escalate this situation? "It is written in the documents in the vault. We had to move into this—"

"Museum? Is that the word you're searching for? Archie explained all that, but he's another thing that threatens Sam. He's the only magic cat I've ever met, but he seems to have a lot of control over these situations, don't you think? Did Aunt Eli really allow this? I don't know, James. The more I learn, the less I like him." She shivered.

"Yeah, well, I'm sorry, but it doesn't work that way." He winced at her scowl. It wasn't what she wanted to hear, he got that, but he had to keep trying. "Archie is Archie, and he comes with the estate. It's a blessing and a curse."

And this day it was mostly a curse. He took Carol by the shoulders, but she pushed him away and turned her back to him.

"So how did we end up in this crucial, time-sensitive, pivotal moment once again?" She froze and spun to face him. "You don't have to leave again, do you?"

How did he tell this woman who held his heart in her hands that he had to do that very thing to save the child that held both of their hearts? "It's out of my control. Nicole—" He watched her face as she scowled in his direction, not meeting his eyes.

"That's just it. We have no control over this, so how are we supposed to protect Sam, let alone Nicole?" She sank onto her haunches and slid to the floor, her back against the mirror.

James joined her on the floor. He couldn't lose her, but he might. Tension vibrated in the air. He sent up a silent prayer to Aunt Eli, as though that might help.

He took Carol's hand. It shook in his. He turned her palm gently in his hands and kissed it. "I'll fix this."

But how? He had no idea, but he had to try.

"What about Archie? Is he going to help?"

"Shhh." James glanced over his shoulder.

"Are you afraid of him? Moving to this house was supposed to be a change for Sam, to help her recover. She still has nightmares, you know." She cocked her head at him.

He hung his head. "I know, and yes. I'm a little bit afraid of Archie. His duty was to Aunt Eli. Now he's here to guide us as we go through this transition into the estate and trust." And he is the Protector of the bricks and all the artifacts. But he wasn't going to say that part out loud.

"I don't get it." She waved her hands in the air. "I don't know if I ever will. All I understand is nothing good comes from those bricks." She put her face in her hands.

He wanted to pull her into his arms, but knew she'd just push him away.

She glanced up, a tear trickling down her face. "Let's just get through today, okay?"

James nodded and stood. He glanced down the hall as Archie peeled away from the wall on the landing and glided with silent footsteps down the spiral stairs.

****

Sunlight streamed through the windows of the sun porch and warmed the carpet on the upstairs landing. Archie licked his paws. He didn't mind waiting, but his ears pricked as he blinked his eyes. The door clicked open, and James emerged from the bedroom. Whatever excuse he'd given Carol had to be enough for now.

Archie sneezed twice as he transformed into human form, wincing a bit. "Time to get to work."

James nodded, and Archie jogged down the spiral stairs to the main entry with James right behind him. They crossed the dark gray marble star in the center of the circular entry and trotted down the second set of spiral stairs. So many circles. So many symbols.

Archie rubbed his lower back as it spasmed. He'd

been standing over the mahogany table for hours since Nicole's letter had arrived. He rolled his shoulders as James strode into the throne room and glanced at Aunt Eli's chair. Did he expect her to be sitting there and save him from this debacle? James still missed her, but he had to accept his fate, or the power of the bricks would succeed straight to Sam, if they hadn't already. Had James forgotten that part of Mistress Eli's explanation? They both knew that Sam wasn't ready.

James joined Archie at the table, raking his fingers through his hair. "This is destroying my family, and I won't tolerate it, bricks or no bricks. I love that woman more than this life."

Archie focused on not lifting his finger from the page as he scrolled down the branches of Nicole's family tree. "I was in the hallway. I heard you, and I remember what Mistress Elise said to you. Do you?"

"You were eavesdropping. I saw you. That means you heard what Carol said, too." James balled his fists at his side

Archie tilted his head. "I am aware." He had better prepare two doses of the *Glemme* potion today, or it would be too late. He wriggled his nose. "I am aware of everything."

James spun and marched up the stairs.

Archie pushed away from the table. He entered the vault and opened the wooden door to an ancient cabinet. He pulled out several glass vials and laid them on a velvet-covered table. He took down a teacup from a shelf and pulled the tiny applicator from the first vial. He let a single drop fall into the cup.

****

Archie hesitated at the top of the stairs. The star

shone radiant in the marble floor. He glanced to the left across the entry to James's office. He'd left Carol a cup of tea by her bedside. She'd assume it was from James as a peace offering. At least that was the plan. He crossed over the marble star floor in the entry and tapped on the office door. Now to immobilize James.

"Enter." James sat at his desk. A streetlamp shone outside the window, creating a silhouette of the new Guardian of the artifacts in the dimly lit room. Archie carried the teacup across the room.

"May I join you?"

James nodded. Archie placed the teacup across from James, who lifted it as he had so many times before. Archie's nose twitched as the scent of Valarian root hit his nostrils. Combined with the other ingredients, James would be out long enough for—

He pushed that thought from his mind. Sam needed his help, and James was too emotional. If James interrupted her jump—

Archie crossed his legs. "You are not the only one to lose a child. Remember Bertha?"

James sat upright in his chair. "Don't you dare mention Bertha to me. I heard the stories, and Aunt Elise told me about the potion, so don't even think of it."

Archie wiggled his nose and blinked. He glanced at the half-empty teacup on the desk. Was it enough?

Archie turned to stare at the empty spot on the bookshelf where the Family Bible should be. It was in the throne room in use for this case. "I try not to think too much on any one thing. I'm driven to do whatever it takes to keep the spacetime continuum in balance, remember? I'm a cat, the Protector. I can't bring myself to—"

James lifted the cup to his lips and took another drink. He settled the cup in the saucer and stared at it. "You didn't—"

"Let me finish." Archie stood and glared at James. "I do care. I cared about Guillem, and all the Guardians through the ages, and I cared about Aunt Elise." Archie sank onto the edge of the chair.

James blinked, but he slumped back into the chair. He held up the cup and sniffed it, then glowered at Archie. "What have you done—"

It was working faster than he expected. A single tear ran down James's cheek. He placed a hand to James' forehead as the man closed his eyes and slumped back in the chair. "And I care about you and Sam now. I would never hurt you, and I only do this out of necessity."

"Mmphllpmm." James' eyes closed, and his mouth gaped open.

"I will take care of her, James." Archie stood. "Now the real work begins."

Chapter Fifteen

Townhouses rose four and five stories above the sidewalk and faced a grassy park. Sam gawked at the ornate carvings on the buildings shading the road. Rich people lived here. Trees lined the park side of the street. *That must be Lincoln's Inn Fields.* Wilbert and Graham walked side-by-side down Great Queen Street. Were they getting close to Darlene's house? Sam gripped Nicole's hand as they trailed behind the men. Was Nicole slowing down?

A breeze lifted Sam's hair. The stench of rotten fish no longer hung in the air, and hints of fresh juniper teased her nostrils. Sam filled her lungs with sweet, fragrant air. All they'd had to do was cross a road and walk around a corner to Nirvana. The difference in the street, the houses, the flowers scenting the air was like night and day.

Sam and Nicole fell behind, but Graham and Wilbert never turned around to check on them, so deep were they in their animated discussion. Were they arguing about Darlene? She'd heard that name several times.

Nicole tripped. Sam clasped her arm, but her friend's pale face startled her, and a quiver rippled through her stomach. Nicole clung to her hand and took one awkward step, then another. Nicole grunted and pushed herself forward. Not even clenching her teeth could stop the buzz in Sam's head.

A gasp escaped Nicole's lips as she dropped to the sidewalk. She's sick. Was it the letter? What else could it be? Sam sank to her side and crouched beside her. She placed an arm around Nicole's shoulders.

"Nicole, talk to me. Tell me what hurts." Sam turned to see Wilbert and Graham still walking and talking.

What the heck?

"Stop, Wilbert. We need a little help?" She stood unsure if she should run after them or stay with her friend. She shook a fist at them, then turned to Nicole. What should she do? She bent down beside her friend.

"Do not pass out. Do you hear me?" Why was she so pale? Was her name disappearing? She stared from Nicole to Graham and Wilbert. *What jerks.* She paced the sidewalk, then crouched down to take Nicole's clammy hand. Nicole never had clammy hands.

Clammy isn't a good sign.

A sob formed in her throat, and she pressed it down. Nicole swayed, and Sam plopped beside her on the sidewalk. What would she say if some rich person came along? Why didn't Graham and Wilbert come back? Were they trying to abandon them?

Closing her eyes, she pictured the map on the mahogany table in the throne room. If they were on Great Queen Street, they must be near Darlene's house, right?

A shadow fell beside her, and she ducked.

"She needs water," a voice said.

Sam threw her arms around Nicole to protect her, but Nicole only stared at her shoes, too exhausted to look up.

"Archie?" Sam pulled her arms from Nicole. "Perfect timing, but don't sneak around like that." She jabbed a finger at him. "And we've lost Graham and

Wilbert."

"Let them go. We need to focus on Nicole. She's suffering the effects of an artifact." Archie opened a canteen in his hand and dribbled water over Nicole's lips. "She's also dehydrated. It can happen quickly when you leap through time."

Nicole swallowed.

He was right. Nicole needed help, and Archie would know what to do. He was the protector after all. Nicole choked but drank all the water Archie offered.

Sam's throat tightened with thirst. "Is there—"

Archie held out the canteen. She took it, guzzling until drops ran down her chin. She wiped her lips. "So, it's an artifact, as in the letter?"

Archie screwed the lid on the canteen. "We must move Nicole off the street so we can talk. Wilbert and Graham will come back for you."

Sam bit her lip. "What's wrong with Nicole?" She put a hand to her chest.

Archie blinked, then began. "A name has disappeared. She must go home and recoup."

"Recoup? But—"

"I must return her to the throne room where I have the tinctures that will help her recover enough to return and complete the mission."

"Tinctures? I'm going too, right?" She couldn't stay here without Nicole. "I need to stick with Nicole." She followed every move he made as she clenched and unclenched her fists. "Don't make me beg, but I'll beg if I have to."

Archie wrinkled his brow as he stole a glance at Nicole. "I have a plan, but first we must get Miss Blevins off the street." He bent to take Nicole's shoulders. "You lift her feet. Careful now."

Sam lifted Nicole's feet as Archie carried her head and shoulders. He lumbered to a vacant townhouse and began climbing the stairs to the front door. The paint was peeling, and a windowpane was cracked, and another was missing glass. Nicole was out cold, and Sam's throat constricted. *What is happening to Nicole?*

Archie hobbled up the final stairs and cradled Nicole in one arm so he could open the faded front door. Nicole moaned, and Sam winced as she cradled her friend's feet. Archie carried Nicole into a drawing room with no furniture. The bitter aroma of cat urine and dust hanging in the air.

Archie stopped in a corner where some packing material of straw and cotton had been piled. He laid Nicole on it with her head well supported, and Sam lowered Nicole's feet.

"What is this place?" Sam stood and jammed her hands on her hips.

Archie cleared his throat. "A home of someone I know. It's a safe place for our conversation."

She didn't want to ask if the friend was dead or alive because she feared the latter. "So, talk. Why didn't Dad come?" Sam blinked back tears. "He promised—"

"He can't join us right now. Nicole activated the portal this time, and you had to follow her. Now we must find a way to rectify whatever Charles has done in London that has sparked changes in Nicole's future. We don't want Nicole to fully disappear. That's a real bugger to reverse."

"What?" Sam wiped her hands over her face, but it didn't wipe what was happening away, and Archie only intensified her fears. "For the love of—"

She sank down beside Nicole and ran her hand over the curls that covered her head. Nicole's warmth radiated to her hand, and Sam locked her gaze on Archie. "Tell me what I have to do?"

"I'll return Nicole to the throne room, and you will find Graham and Wilbert to help you locate Darlene. Is that clear?"

"Without Nicole? Won't they know something is wrong?"

"Something is wrong. Nicole is disappearing. Her name was almost gone when I left."

"Where's Dad? Why didn't he come?"

"He's more a danger to you, right now, than an asset." Archie tensed his shoulders. "I've seen it before with Mistress Elise."

"What?" Sam froze, her arms growing leaden. Was he obtuse because he was a cat, or was he trying to hurt her? "Which Elise?"

"You are living in her house." Archie cocked an eyebrow at her. "When Bertha disappeared, she wanted to leap through time without preparing. Because of how Bertha had triggered the bricks without an artifact, if the mistress had tried to find Bertha, they both could have been lost, and the negative energy it took for two unsuccessful leaps would have permanently warped the time-space—"

"For the love of—" Sam grabbed Archie's coat. "How do we save Nicole?" She released him.

"Graham holds the key. He loves Darlene, but she leaves for America soon. Something is changing between them, and whatever it is will spark a chain of events that will wipe a whole branch of Nicole's family out of existence, including her."

Sam shut her eyes. "Her family tree. I can recall every name."

"That's why I asked you to run your finger over all the names. Touching them embedded them into your memory, and we need that knowledge now."

"Well, why didn't you just say so?"

"Would you have believed me?" He stared at her without blinking. "Repeat the list beginning with Freddie, I mean Frederick Wilhelm Meyer II."

Sam stared into space. The names appeared before her and she recited, "Frederick II marries Constance and gives birth to Darlene. They have two more children that do not survive their first year." She stopped. "Why is this relevant?" She glanced at Nicole lying on the floor. Her face was pasty white, and her chest rose and fell in shallow breaths.

"Because Frederick is Freddie from Portland, and there's a third element."

Sam held her hand out and grabbed the fireplace mantel. The room spun. "No. It can't be."

"Yes. Mr. Stickel has threatened Freddie and his family for money, again, so Freddie planned to escape him by taking his family to Seattle. Unfortunately, Stickel has been using the bricks to confuse the family and interfere with their departure." Archie knelt beside Nicole.

"Stickel." Sam ground her teeth and peered at Archie.

Archie nodded and stared into her eyes. "Do you want your friend to live?"

"Of course, but I don't understand. He was in Seattle. How did he return?"

"It's a long story, but suffice it to say, Darlene's

relationship with Graham was affected by Stickel threatening her father, Frederick Meyer III, you knew him as Freddie, and Freddie's refusal to pay has made Stickel desperate. Freddie's departure is imminent now, and thus, Darlene never marries—"

"Graham." She knelt beside Nicole. "So, how do we fix this?"

"What is today?" Archie shut his eyes and tapped his chin. "Right. It's September 30th, a Tuesday." Archie placed a hand on Sam's. "If we don't stop Stickel, Nicole doesn't stand a chance."

Sam bit her lip. "Stop him? That's the plan?"

"Yes, for now it is. Freddie booked passage on tomorrow's voyage to New York. It's the last sailing of the season and Freddie's last opportunity to escape his uncle. If Stickel kidnaps Darlene, which is my fear, Freddie will never leave Darlene behind, which means he won't leave London. In that scenario, Stickel wins."

Sam put a hand to her forehead. Could this get any more complicated? "So how did he get to London? Was that what started Nicole's family names disappearing?"

"Yes. A modern Seattle did not suit Mr. Stickel, and he wanted revenge on Freddie for the banking debacle in Portland. He figured out a way to return to his own time. But once the letter arrived at Nicole's, I was able to locate his current location in London near Freddie's townhouse across from Lincoln's Inn Fields." Archie inhaled.

Sam waited. "Go on." How could he be so calm while Mr. Stickel was destroying Nicole's life?

Archie cleared his throat. "His latest desire, besides ruining Freddie, is to buy a theater and be an actor on the stage. That is what drives him, but Freddie and

Constance had made plans to move to Seattle. Freddie has hired an architect to draw up plans and build the house in which you now reside."

Sam gasped. "The museum?"

Archie blinked, then continued. "Yes. He purchased a plot in Seattle on Queen Ann Hill before he left Portland. He and Constance decided to live in England until Darlene became of age and her elderly parents passed on. But Stickel arrived and might just spoil their plan if he gets his way."

"Wait a minute. It was the land on Queen Anne Hill, right? We have the same star as Grandma Meyer had in her entry." Would this nightmare ever end?

Archie glanced down at Nicole. "The sooner you find Graham, the sooner you can help Darlene before she departs. I'm not sure of the specifics, but a plan will reveal itself to you."

"Oh, will it now?" Sam shook her head.

Archie opened the door and motioned for her to go. "You must hurry."

Sam locked eyes on Nicole's form one last time, then turned and jogged down the steps. She scanned down the road as far as she could as she dodged a nanny pushing a pram, and a couple strolling arm and arm. Graham and Wilbert were running straight for her. She waved. Maybe the solution *would* present itself, but how?

Graham pointed. "There she is." They ran up to her, breathing hard.

"Where did you two go off to? We turned around and you were gone." Wilbert scanned the street. "Where's Nicole?"

The wild look in Wilbert's eyes surprised her.

Archie had said her job was to help Graham find Darlene, right? But Wilbert seemed more distraught over her imminent departure. Was he the letter writer?

Chapter Sixteen

Church bells rang, and Sam glanced at Graham, who shook his head at Wilbert. Why was he angry?

Graham jabbed a finger at Wilbert. "That's three o'clock, mate."

"Graham, listen—"

"No. St. Anselm and St. Cecilia always ring true. Darlene is in trouble. I'll never get to say goodbye now."

Sam stepped away from Graham as the crowds on the streets milled and meandered up to the church steps and inside. It must be afternoon mass, or something, because every wife and mother in the neighborhood was out.

Before she could make up a lie about Nicole, Graham turned and disappeared in the crowd in front of the church. She raised a hand, but Wilbert too was soon enveloped by the crowd as he rushed after Graham. She was alone.

She wrapped her arms around her torso. At least she didn't have to add another lie to her list. The noise, the crowds, and the chaos overpowered her sense of equilibrium. She backed into a building, put her hands to her head, and closed her eyes. If only she could disappear or jump home. Where was Dad when she needed him?

"Dang him." She'd have to figure this out on her own. She rushed down the street until she came to Bow Street. She rubbed her eyes. What did she do now? Go back to where she'd first landed in Covent Garden. Yes. The toy shop. She inhaled and exhaled, then turned right on Bow and jogged until she found Floral. She wended down a wide alley until it opened into the market, and she meandered through flowers, pots and pans, and cheese stalls. Wilbert and Graham had led them through this very street earlier. She wiped her brow and scanned another row of shops. A cheerful red sign with white lettering proclaimed, "Peebles' Pretties Toy Shoppe." She crossed the street and entered the shop.

"Here is your package, Miss Meyer." An ancient clerk behind the counter handed a young woman a brightly wrapped package.

Miss Meyer? Sam froze and stared at the young woman the clerk had addressed. Was this Nicole's grandma? Had she found Darlene?

"Thank you, Mr. Partridge. I can't believe you received this so soon. We leave for America tomorrow, you know." She took the package and walked to the door.

Sam turned to a shelf. Tomorrow? They were running out of time. Archie was right, the artifacts were directing her instincts, and now she could follow Darlene home, but then what? Maybe when they got close to Lincoln's Inn Fields, she could approach her with the news of Graham and a secret meeting. Was that too creepy? Maybe it shouldn't be secret, but urgent. She'd have to think of something—

She bit her knuckle. She'd gotten burned acting before thinking in Portland, but she had to sort out the letter debacle with Darlene before she and her family departed for America, Sam was sure of it.

Darlene strolled out of the toy shop and down the road to a tea shop. Sam hung back, trying to keep her distance and not act too stalker-like. Darlene entered the shop and took a seat. Really? How long was this going to take? Sam paced on the street in front of the shop. Maybe this was her chance to strike up a conversation or—

She stopped. If Graham was the letter writer, this shop could be the perfect place for Graham to meet with her, but how did Sam make that happen? She peered through the dirty glass window as Darlene lifted a fork and took a dainty bite of a tiny petit four. Aunt Eli loved the tiny decorative cakes, and Sam's mouth watered. Why was she so hungry? She was not dressed nice enough to join her for tea in this lovely shop. Darlene's hat alone must have cost a fortune, let alone the rust colored fitted jacket and matching dress.

"What are you doing here?" Graham asked, rushing up behind her.

Sam jumped and spun around. "How—"

Graham caught her as she wobbled. Archie was right. The solution did present itself. Here was Graham, but she'd almost had a stroke. She put a hand to her chest.

"You startled me. Don't sneak up on a person."

Graham ignored her. "I can't find Darlene. I'm still—"

Sam shook her head. "She's inside." She pointed at Darlene sitting at a table inside the shop. "She's—"

"Darlene? Where is Nurse?" Graham dropped her arm and peered through the window.

"Nurse? Is she sick?" Sam peered through the window, looking for signs of illness.

"What? No. Her nanny is called Nurse." Graham's lip curled as he snorted.

"How old is—"

Graham ignored her. "How do I tell her? I wrote this silly letter, but—" He patted the pocket of his jacket and wrung his hands.

Sam shook her head. "What are you saying? You're not going with her, and you wrote a letter telling her?" Sam's jaw dropped. His body odor hit her like a cloud. Ugh. When did they invent deodorant?

Graham shuddered a sigh. "My uncle is dying, and her uncle is making life impossible for her father. That's why they have to leave immediately. What is it with uncles anyway?" Graham gazed at the tea shop. "I have to say my goodbyes now or at least give her my letter."

"Hmm." Sam didn't know what to say. She had seen Graham's name in the family Bible, hadn't she? This changed everything.

He hung his head and shook it. "You found her, which gives me the chance I was hoping for. Thank you." He bowed, then strode into the shop.

Darlene stood, almost tipping the table in her haste. Graham took her hand and kissed it, and Sam ducked behind a cart. Darlene sat again with Graham and their heads bent together, her face blotched and wet from tears.

Now what did she do? Spy on them? No. She'd head back to the house where Archie had taken Nicole, but had she accomplished their goal? Did this solve the problem?

****

The steps creaked and groaned as Sam climbed to the front door one at a time. She paused. Was that Archie's voice? She knocked on the door, and Archie cracked it and pulled her inside. Nicole was still lying where they'd placed her when they carried her into this room, and she gave her a weak wave.

Archie placed a hand on her shoulder. "You did well, Sam. Nicole woke eight minutes ago."

"That would be when Darlene hugged him. Oh man, it's working." Sam raked her fingers through her hair. She sank down beside Nicole, who nursed the canteen of water.

"I think we are finished here. We can all head back together if you'd like."

"I'd like." Nicole sighed and handed the canteen to Sam.

"Me too. I'm so relieved. Did you know Darlene would be at the toy shop?"

"What?" Archie seemed distracted.

Sam's stomach tightened. "What do you mean, what?"

"Where did you leave Darlene and Wilbert?"

"Wilbert? It was Graham, and I left them at a tea shop on Market."

"Graham? Are you certain?"

"Pretty certain." Sam's stomach tightened, and she stared at Archie. "Why?"

"Graham's name has disappeared. He might not have been the letter writer. You must get back there." Archie opened the door. "Report back as soon as you can."

Sam blinked back tears. "He just told me he isn't going with Darlene. Is that why his name disappeared?"

Archie scratched his chin, staring into the distance. "He told you that?"

"He did, but what—"

"Something else is going on here. It must be Stickel who—"

"Stickel?"

"He's at it again." Archie's expression left no doubt that he was serious.

****

Sam sprinted down the stairs, past the church, and down an alley. She dodged through the crowds, retracing her steps to the tea shop and skidded to a stop. No. A crowd had gathered in the street. A shudder ran through her, and she stood frozen. It was him.

A short stocky man in a trim jacket and creased slacks held Darlene by the elbow. It was Stickel. Freddie lay sprawled on the sidewalk. Graham must have left before Darlene's dad arrived, or—

She backed into a vestibule and watched as people walked past the scene, staring. Mr. Stickel shooed them away.

"Father, oh, Father. Are you hurt?" Darlene jerked her arm away from Mr. Stickel, but Stickel hung on. "Uncle Charles. Unhand me this instant."

"Now, now, niece. You must return home with me. Until your father agrees to my terms, you will stay with me." Mr. Stickel nodded to a man who nodded back with approval.

Sam had to do something. Freddie had a boat to catch, and Darlene was in the clutches of a madman.

"Uncle Charles, no. Father."

Stickel tried to pull Darlene away from Freddie's unconscious body, but she pulled back, refusing to move. Sam inched closer.

He grimaced. "I'm going to tell your mother about this unless you—"

"You leave Mother out of this. You've hurt Pappa, and you aren't supposed to be near me or my family."

The more Darlene protested, the larger the crowd grew. She had to do something, now.

"Excuse me, aren't you Mr. Charles Mortimer Stickel, Esq.?" She pushed her way through the crowd and came up behind Mr. Stickel.

"Why yes I am." He turned to see who was speaking. "Wha-wha-wha—"

He dropped Darlene's arm, and she bent over Freddie, who had fallen on her package. She pulled out a hanky and wiped his face and held his hand.

"You." Mr. Stickel's face went from white to red.

Sam turned and ran. Mr. Stickel's lumbering footsteps echoed off the shop walls as he chased her. She chuckled. That went as planned, but what now?

She dodged in and out of carts until she couldn't hear his labored breathing anymore. She circled back and made her way to the corner where she'd left Freddie on the ground with Darlene hovering over him. The corner was empty. She scanned the Market and all the streets and alleys.

A rust-colored hat disappeared around a corner and Sam sprinted across the street. She could catch them if—

"Oy, boyo, want to meet your maker, eh?" A cart driver shook his fist at her as he drove between her and where Darlene's hat had disappeared around the corner.

She wanted to correct the man, but could only raise a hand as the man made a "V" sign with his knuckles facing her. What did that mean? By the expression on the man's face, nothing good. She dashed after Darlene in time to see her helping Freddie into the toy shop. At least father and daughter were together.

Sam paused. Now what? Did she follow, or report back to Archie?

She snuck into Peebles' Pretties and down to the stockroom. Maybe she'd come up with a plan—

Wilbert cleared his throat, and she spun. He met her at the bottom of the stairs.

"Hello, you." He took off his hat and looked past her.

Did he expect Graham and Darlene?

"I got a call about a break-in at this address and found the door unlocked." He frowned. "You'd better tell me what's going on, and you better start with the truth."

Chapter Seventeen

The familiar scent of lavender filled Nicole's nostrils as she cracked open her eyelids. Archie was hovering over her and patting her face to wake her. She grabbed his hand and opened her eyes wider. Dust motes floated through the light beams streaming through the stained-glass windows. The throne room?

The silence in the house comforted her as he fluffed a pillow under her head. She lay on the overstuffed burgundy couch Aunt Eli had bought at the antique market. She spared no expense on her furnishings, and the couch was no different. The carved mahogany legs and arms set it apart from more contemporary designs. She ran her hand over the pattern in the upholstery fabric, a subtle nod to the French fleur-de-lis.

She pushed to sit. "Ugh." She put a hand to her head, then rested back on the pillow.

"No sudden moves, Miss Nicole." Archie's voice was quiet. Was that concern in his voice? He'd been such a jerk in Portland, but he was on her side now. She was getting used to his blunt behavior and unblinking eyes.

She rubbed her temples. "Why did you bring me here?" The aroma of lavender filled the air along with the tang of ozone. "Where is Sam?" Nicole managed to sit as Archie helped her.

"You were comatose. I had no choice." Archie rubbed his hands together.

"But Sam—"

"—has work to do to make sure you stay healthy." He held her wrist. Was he taking her pulse?

She pulled her hand away. "You left Sam alone in London? We have to go back. Now." She tried to sit but fell back against the cushion.

He shook his head. "You don't have the strength. It's up to Sam now. She has Wilbert and Graham, and once you're—"

"But until then, she's alone." Nicole clamped her fingers on the edge of the table. He was right. The room was spinning, and she'd never make it two steps in London. "Fine."

He stood and walked to the large table opposite the open vault door.

"Does anyone ever lock that vault? It's filled with valuable magic stuff. Anyone could take it."

"They'd have to get past me." He stood his full five feet and nine inches. "It stays open when there is a case under investigation, like now. Hopefully, we experience a quick resolution."

"So, I have a case?" Nicole followed Archie with her gaze.

He pulled his collar away from his throat and his Adam's apple bobbed. "Precisely."

She swung her feet to the floor and stopped as the room spun. "Whoa." She was so dizzy.

He stared at her with unblinking amber eyes. "Time travel is hard on the body and the mind, as you are finding out, but in your case, the issue we are working on and the reason the vault is open is because of disappearing names in your family tree." He turned and opened a book.

"Names disappearing again?" She stood and walked to the table on legs that wobbled.

"They are."

"Is Sam okay?" She put a hand to her chest as her heart threatened to beat out of her ribs. She couldn't seem to catch her breath.

"Sam is fine. She is helping to solve your problem." He turned and the steady beam of his amber eyes hit her like a slap to the face.

She blinked. "Is Mom okay?" She wrung her hands together. "Are my family names disappearing?"

Archie folded his hands and stood with them clasped in front of him. He nodded.

Nicole scanned the room. "How is this happening?"

"It's a long story." He cleared his throat. "I'd better make a pot of yerba-mate."

****

The stockroom light flickered as Sam stood pressed against the wall. Dust tickled her nose, and she put her face in her elbow as a sneeze burst from her. She glanced at Wilbert. He hadn't moved. Could he handle the truth?

"Don't give me a load of tosh." He paced the narrow aisle. "And don't tell me you need to see a man about a dog. I know you're in trouble." He shrugged. "I want to help you and Nicole."

"A man about a what?" She stared at him.

Where did she begin? With Mr. Stickel's a time-traveler, and they needed to catch him before Nicole disappeared? She had to tell him something because he wasn't going to let her complete her mission until she did.

She raised her hands as if to hold him off. "Okay, okay. It's true. I haven't been totally honest with you.

Nicole is related to Darlene, but she isn't her cousin. We're from the future, hence the weird clothes." She'd better let that settle in his brain.

Wilbert didn't blink. He didn't move. He opened his mouth, but no sound came out. At least he wasn't laughing at her or hauling her back to Bow Street Station.

"Nicole is from—"

"The future. It's a family problem. It has to do with some Roman bricks, some books, and artifacts."

"You mean like archeology?" His face was pale.

She tilted her head. That could explain it. "Yes. Like archeology, but more complicated. It involves our ancestors." She paused. He hadn't run away, so that was good. She took a breath and continued. "We time-traveled, which takes magic artifacts active by sanquis familiae, which means family blood. The artifacts create a portal." She stopped to take a breath. Archie might be proud that she'd remembered the Latin, but was Wilbert? She pressed her hand to her chest. Did he believe her? He was still here.

He scratched his head. "Does Darlene use magic artifacts to create portals?"

Sam did a double-take. Was he trying to understand? That was a good sign, right? "I don't think so, but I guess in theory she could. I know her father, Mr. Meyer, has used them."

"That would explain why Mr. Meyer's trips to America were so short." He scanned the room.

"Mr. Charles Stickel has also been known to use the bricks. The last time I saw him was in Portland, 1901."

"Wha-wha—" Wilbert's eyes bulged, and his mouth gaped open.

"Nicole and I have jumped through time before, but

I still don't know everything about it." Sam rolled her sleeves to her elbows, then clasped her hands together. She might as well tell him everything, but he was growing pale. Was he going to pass out? She waited for him to speak.

He leaned a hand against the wall to support himself. "Is that why Nicole seemed so confused when I found her in the Peebles' Pretties Toy Shoppe stockroom?"

"Yes. We have a new artifact, a letter, but I think it got lost in the mail and wasn't found until our time when it arrived at Nicole's in a Royal Mail envelope. That letter sparked all of this." She waved her hand through the air.

"So, you're a magician then?"

"No. Not a magician."

He gasped and backed away. "You're fae."

"Fae?"

He stepped away from her, holding up his hands. "You're a wicked faerie."

****

Nicole stood beside Archie at the table. He ran his finger over a branch of the tree and then turned to another page. The ink was faded, and some names weren't legible.

"We should be able to see these names. The good news is they are faint but not gone completely."

Nicole's stomach knotted and she pressed her hands over it. "That's good news? Where is Mr. Stewart?"

Archie lifted his finger from the page and took her hand. He placed her pointer finger on her branch of the family. She pulled her hand back.

"That felt like a shock. What's going on?"

"Sam can save your family names in spite of

Charles, but—"

He put a hand to his mouth. "Oh no."

"What is it?" The room whirled and Nicole clung to the edge of the table for support. If she fell, she might not be strong enough to stand again.

Archie took her by the elbow and walked her to the couch. Was he pale? His red hair had a washed-out look, and the freckles across his nose looked darker. He sank down on the sofa beside her.

"I must check something. You rest." He moved to the table and pulled out a map and the family Bible. He ran his finger over the map, then turned to a family tree. Was it hers?

"It's Charles. Sam failed to—"

Nicole pushed to a wobbly stand. "Stickel's in London, and you left Sam there?" She glared at him.

Chapter Eighteen

The scent of lavender hit Carol's nostrils as she entered the throne room. "Is James down here?" She rubbed her eyes. The aromas were steaming from the bowls on a monstrous mahogany table where Archie stood.

"So, what do I do? How can I help? What are you doing?"

He stared at her unblinking. "Come here. You need to see this."

She leaned over the table to see what he was pointing at. "I don't see anything?"

Nicole rose from the couch and wobbled to her side. "Please, Mrs. Stewart."

She gasped. "Oh, Nicole, honey, I didn't see you there under all those blankets." How had she not noticed Nicole, and she was pale as death? "You're not well." She reached for Nicole's arm and guided her back to the couch.

A shiver ran the length of her body. What was she doing? She promised herself that she wasn't going to lose control of her emotions. She sank beside Nicole on the couch.

Nicole's bloodshot eyes searched her own. "No. I'm not well. Sam and Archie are helping me, and even though I'm getting stronger every minute, Sam is doing what I should be doing. I should be out there saving my family right now, not her."

"Sam is what, now?" Carol's stomach flipped, and she shook her head. "How can Sam—" She gasped and spun to face Archie. "But—" She rose into a crouch.

Nicole took Carol's hand in hers and gave a tug.

Carol sank back onto the couch at Nicole's touch.

"I wouldn't even exist anymore if it wasn't for Sam."

"What?" Carol's head pivoted from Nicole to Archie. "Is this true?"

Archie shrugged. "Sam is your daughter, and you might not want to hear this right now, but Nicole's very existence was at stake."

Nicole cleared her throat and, with a weak grasp, squeezed Carol's hand. My God, they were telling her the truth.

Nicole stared at Carol, then stood. "Please, Mrs. Stewart. Don't be mad at Archie. He gave Sam instructions on what to do to save my family, and she's doing it. She's saving my life too." Nicole raised her shoulders in a small shrug. Every movement was an effort for the girl.

She glanced at the stairs as James jogged into the room. "What's going on?"

"Good grief." Carol rushed to him. "Why didn't you say Nicole was hurt?"

James took her by the shoulders. "Carol—"

Carol threw up her hands, blocking his grip. "Are you all conspiring against my sanity? Nicole—"

She scrubbed her face with both hands and took a deep breath to fill her lungs. She dropped her hands to her sides. "This is a lot to process." She turned and headed to the stairs. Nicole needed sustenance. Would chicken soup help? All she knew was, no one was going to solve anything on an empty stomach.

She blew a hiss of air through her pursed lips. This was what happened when a magic cat was in charge. Protector? Really?

****

Wilbert paced on one side of the room, as far away from Sam as possible. She didn't blame him. It was a lot to take in at first, but he hadn't hauled her to the insane asylum. Yet. Did he believe her, though?

"So, you're sure you aren't a faerie, but you can travel through time, and you are here because Nicole, who is also from the future, got a letter from London in this time with only the initials D and G to identify the correspondents, and it had Peebles' Pretties Toy Shoppe's address on it? When was it dated?"

Sam put a hand to her lips. "1929? Yes, I believe it was." Was this him believing her? He hadn't clapped handcuffs on her and marched her to jail yet.

"So." He scratched his head. "Is that everything?"

"Almost. I must help Darlene and her family escape Mr. Charles Mortimer Stickel Esq. from doing whatever it is he is doing because that is what is changing the future." She gestured with her pointer finger to the door. "He wants to abduct her, you know, and I might still be able to catch—"

Wilbert stared at her and held up a hand. "He's a respectable banker, isn't he? Isn't Darlene's father also a bank—"

"Yes, and yes." She clasped her hands. "Stickel embezzled money from his bank—"

"I did not know—"

"And he wants a loan from Fre—Mr. Meyer, who

won't loan one cent to the embezzler."

Wilbert stared at her as if she had two heads. "Wait a minute. He stole money from his family's bank before, and now he's trying to do it again?"

"Among other things."

"Do you have proof?"

"Well." Sam scratched her head. It all sounded so crazy, but how did she prove it? She faced Wilbert and continued. "Please bear with me, but I speak the truth." She patted her pockets and pulled out her cell phone. "This is how we communicate. It's a phone." She winced as she kept him in her line of vision and held it out to him.

He leaned over the phone. "Is it a leather-bound tablet?" He backed away from her. How would he take that piece of information?

She pressed her fingers to her temples. This was taking too long. Stickel could have found Darlene by now. "Listen, Graham and Darlene are only part of what is happening. Mr. Stickel can't keep Darlene from traveling to America or bad things will happen. Nicole's entire family will disappear if Stickel isn't stopped."

Wilbert glanced at the ceiling and tapped his chin. "I can't arrest him. You realize that?"

Sam's jaw dropped.

****

Colorful sunlight fell onto the mahogany table. Nicole tried to stand. Her legs were still shaking from the effort, so she clung to the couch for support. James had left to help Carol make dinner, and the aroma of chicken soup wafted down the stairs and into the room. Left alone with Archie, a tightness filled her chest. How did she remain calm in this storm of uncertainty? She wobbled to the glass bookcase doors, reflecting the room. Why was Archie hovering around her?

She stopped. "Are you afraid I'm going to fall?"

He nodded as she moved to the far-left shelf and pulled open a glass door. It opened.

"I thought these doors were kept locked." She turned to Archie. His breath tickled her ear, and she stepped back.

"Only the shelves containing the family bible with all the Greats are ever locked."

She grinned. Sam had called her ancestors "the Greats" since she'd known her, which was forever ago. Did the saying originate from Archie? "Why do you call them 'the Greats'?"

Archie turned to face her. "Because the family traces its origins to Roman times around the 4th century BC. The number of greats used to describe each member becomes confusing, so we just use—"

"The Greats. Got it. Makes total sense. I wish my family went back that far." She let out a sigh and ran her fingers along the leather spines of the books. An energy ran through her fingers as they touched each title, *Exploratio Energia Negative in Corpore Humano* sounded in her mind as if being said aloud. She stared at Archie, who shrugged.

She shook her head, but the words still reverberated in her skull. "What's happening? Is this title in Latin?"

Archie glanced at the title. "Yes. Good job. It translates to, *The Exploration of Negative Energy in the Human Body.* It has to do with time-travel and 'jumping' or 'leaping' as you call it."

Did he just compliment her? This must be a first. A grin spread across her face, and she tried to subdue it.

She stared at the books on the shelf. "I'm getting this. So, time-travel leaves an effect on our bodies when we use the artifacts."

"Indeed. You are astute in your comprehension of these complex ideas." He cocked his head to the side as though confused.

Nicole glared at him. Was he starting her lessons in time-travel and the artifacts? "So I get to take lessons too?"

"Yes. Sam's frightened, so you will be a big influence on her lessons as she will be on yours." Archie cleared his throat and shoved his hands in his pockets.

"Oh. She has been acting weird, but I didn't realize it was because she was afraid." She waited for a response, but Archie just gave a small nod.

She ran her finger over another title. "And this one? *Natura Consanguinea Artificium Activum?*"

He grinned. "Excellent pronunciation. Have you studied Latin?"

She shook her head no.

He translated the title with his hand on his hips. "*The Consanguineal Nature of Activating Artifacts.*"

Nicole chuckled. "Now you're talking. But what does consanguineal mean?"

Archie replied with a twinkle in his amber eye. "That is the key to all of this. It is what brought me into existence as an immortal creature, what activates the bricks and every artifact that came after them. It is the family blood." He stopped his gaze on her face as he nodded.

She squirmed under his close observation. What did he see, and why was he nodding? She put a hand to her throat and gasped. "Wait. So, what Sam told me is true?

I have the family blood, too? So, Sam and I—"

Archie grinned. "Precisely, my dear girl. Welcome to the family."

Chapter Nineteen

James came down with several bowls of chicken noodle soup, steam wafting from the tray, the aroma making her stomach rumble.

He placed the tray on the couch. "Eat up. We have work to do."

Carol followed with a pitcher of ice water and several glasses on another tray.

Nicole took the bowl James offered her. She adjusted her seat on the couch so she could perch it on her knees as she propped a pillow behind her back. She glanced from Carol to James. "Sam is your daughter. I get it, but I don't know what to say about how to fix this. I'm not the Protector or the Guardian of anything." She sank into the corner of the couch and took a spoonful of soup.

Archie cleared his throat. "This situation is dangerous for me. You must remember, I only have two more lives, and Sam—"

The whole room shook, and Archie clutched the edge of the table. "No, no, no." He glanced from James to Nicole. "He's at it again."

Nicole leapt from the couch and scanned the books and map on the table. "Who? You don't mean Stickel, do you?"

Carol joined her and put a hand on her shoulder as she wobbled, her heart ratcheting against her ribs. "Sam.

Is she okay?"

"If we don't stop Charles once and for all, we could lose Sam as well."

****

The stock room walls seemed to close in on her. The rows of shelves with boxes of toys, large and small and covered in dust, made Sam's eyes swim. She blinked. *Was that—*

Stickel stepped out of the shadows in the back of the cellar. Sam put a hand to her mouth, but no sound came out.

Wilbert scoffed. "Don't tell me you can read minds, too? Tell me wha—"

Stickel grabbed Wilbert's club from his belt and a loud pop rang out as he cracked Wilbert on the skull. He spun to glare at Sam. "You. You will pay for what you've done to me, first in Portland, and now here." He shook the club at Sam. "Your tiresome meddling ends now."

Wilbert lay sprawled at her feet. Now what was she supposed to do? The shine in Stickel's eyes grew brighter as he glared at her. She inched toward the stairs.

"Tell me where she is, or I'll—"

"Archie took Nicole home." She raised her hands. How was she supposed to stop Stickel by herself? He was insane.

"Not Nicole, you nincompoop." He raised the club and charged at her.

Sam's reflexes kicked in, and she scrambled for the stairs, reached the top, and fumbled the doorknob.

Stickel clambered up the stairs after her and clobbered her hand.

"Ouch. Stop it." She cradled her hand and glared at

him, backing down the stairs. "What do you—"

"You know what I want." He followed her to the bottom and stood with his legs apart in a fighting stance. "We're all related, you know, so it won't matter if it's you or Darlene."

"I don't—"

"Yes, you do." He laughed and pointed the Billy club at her. "You are the key to all my misfortune, and you are going to pay."

Sam shrank against the door frame. "You are crazy. It's because we are related that I can't tell you. Do you have any idea the damage you are doing to the time-space continuum? You increase the negative energy each time you try to change history." She didn't care if what she said was true or not. "You're a lunatic, and I'm going to stop you from ever hurting another member of my family."

"Your family?" He chuckled until his belly rolled. "Don't you mean our family?"

She held herself upright, but all she wanted to do was collapse. How did Dad do this job? She gritted her teeth and tried again. "You were in Seattle last time I saw you. How did you even get here?"

For a moment, she saw his eyes grow soft, but his features soon hardened into a grimace. "You never cared about me or that I had nowhere to go in Seattle, no friends, not even a warm meal?" He paused. "Even though I had plenty of family, namely you, none of you cared about me at all." He sniffled and peeped at her from under a guarded brow. "I learned a new trick about those bricks."

"But Dad collected them. He said he—"

"He left that task for two weeks before he removed

them. Thanks for not telling him about me." He winked at her.

Sam resisted the urge to slap his face. Why hadn't Dad listened to her when she had told him she thought she'd seen Stickel? He'd probably thought she was hallucinating and chalked it up to her PTSD from the Portland debacle. "But—"

"But nothing." Charles' body shook with another aggravating fit of laughter. "He left the bricks unguarded, and I was able to use them to return to Portland. I came to London the old-fashioned way, on a ship." He stomped his foot. "A lot of good that did me. Freddie refuses to help me. Doesn't family mean anything anymore?"

"What do you want this time? The Alaska Gold Rush is over." Sam squinted at him. Could she hate him any more than she did right now?

"What do I want besides a little revenge? Money, of course. I just need a bit of capital to fund my new theater on Drury Lane. Turns out I'm quite the thespian." He turned a pose and described a flourish with his fingers.

"Thespian? You have got to be kidding me. Time is running out—"

"What?" His focus burned into her.

Heat rose to her cheeks. Had she pushed him too far? How did she explain about the stock market crash of 1929?

"What do you know about time? I have all the time in the world to open my theater, thanks to those bricks." He swung the billy club through the air.

Sam shook her head. He had no idea what the future would bring, but then again, neither did she. Her one goal was to save Nicole, but right now, she had to save herself from this madman.

He fiddled with his tie, his eyes never focusing on one thing. Was this what insanity looked like? He scanned the room and ceiling over and over. Think, Sam, divert his attention.

She folded her arms over her chest. "You'd be surprised what I know." She flashed him what she hoped was a withering glare. Why bother explaining the crash of the stock market? "You're not opening anything."

Wilbert moaned as he pushed himself from the floor. "Unless it's the door to Bedlam."

Mr. Stickel raised his foot to swing a kick at him. This was her chance. She flew into Mr. Stickel, and they both tumbled to the floor. The billy club went flying. Sam jumped away, Mr. Stickel's touch was repulsive to her, and backed toward Wilbert.

Wilbert wiped his eyes.

"Are you okay?" He had to be okay.

Wilbert brushed the dust from his slacks, and Sam kept her eye on Mr. Stickel.

"Mr. Charles Mortimer Stickel Esq., you're under arrest for—"

"No." Mr. Stickel popped up like a Jack-in-the-box and climbed the stairs on his hands and knees. "I won't go to the gaol." He yanked the door open and rushed out into the street with Wilbert hard on his heels.

Sam rushed after them. She picked up her pace so she wouldn't lose Wilbert. She was so close to fixing this, she could feel it, but she needed to contain Stickel for that to happen. Sam rushed through the open door and scanned the street for Mr. Stickel, who disappeared into an alley. Wilbert pumped his arms, trying to catch him.

"No." Sam sank onto the doorstep.

****

The glass doors in the bookcases against the west wall clattered and shook. Nicole stared at the walls and ceiling. The chicken soup had restored some of her energy, but her legs buckled.

"Why is the house shaking?" Her head spun.

Archie took her arm, and she let him lead her to the couch. James stood, his feet braced and his arms out for balance. He rushed into the vault.

She gripped Archie's arm. "Do the bricks cause earthquakes?"

Archie patted her hand and untangled her fingers from his sleeve. "Not in the geological meaning of the word."

She shook her head. What did that even mean? She rubbed her index finger between her eyebrows. "Then what caused the whole house to shake?"

Archie shrugged but avoided eye contact with her. "Stickel still influences the past with his behavior. He must be making a move I didn't account for, or Sam is pushing him to—"

Archie paused.

What was he waiting for? James emerged from the vault and strode to the table. He rested his right hand on the book as lavender filtered through the air.

"Archie's right. It's not geological. It's metaphysical." He stared at the book under his hand. "That wasn't in my mind, though. I shook with the whole house, and I'm worried about Sam." He raked his fingers through his hair.

Nicole pushed to a stand but wobbled and sank back to the couch. Her heart pounded. "Is Carol okay with magic now?"

"Carol is trying to support her daughter as she learns the magic and the time leaps. This, in turn, helps you, but Stickel's constant interference is proving more destructive than I imagined." Archie rubbed his hands together.

She shuddered. He did that every time he was nervous, and he was doing it all the time of late. She ground her teeth, but it didn't calm the quake that moved through her body.

Archie moved toward the vault. "I must leave, even if—"

"I'm going with you." Nicole tried to stand.

"No." Archie blinked twice. "You are too weak."

James sank onto the couch with Nicole and took her hand. He nodded at Archie. "Do what you have to do, just save Sam."

****

Archie landed on all fours. Jumping in cat form was easier for that very reason. The air in the tunnel filled with the bleach-like odor of ozone from the jump, followed by the scent of lavender. He sneezed. Guillem had relied on lavender for all his healing spells. Now Archie had to heal this rift that was causing Nicole's family to disappear.

He licked his left paw as he took in the tunnel and the tracks running down the middle. The Royal Mail Rail tunnel. Maybe he could solve all their problems here if he could find that letter. He sat on his haunches and ran his tongue between his toes. Dirty Mail Rail tunnels. Of course, he'd picked up a sliver. This jump was too important to be injured before he started. He needed all his physical abilities at one hundred percent.

He scanned the tunnel for workers. The rumbling of

a small mail railcar sounded in the distance. If his calculations were correct, this would be where the letter fell from the car. The magic allowed only this one chance for him to catch it because he couldn't replicate this moment in time ever again. He braced himself, ignoring the pain. If he could just catch it and slip it back onto the car somehow, Nicole would recover, and Sam could come home.

The cars rattled around a corner and headed right for him at twenty-five miles per hour. This was it. He saw the end of one bag, its strings dangling out of the car. One letter was inching out of the bag. His joints ached, preparing for the jump he had to make. It tumbled from the bag and floated in the rush of displaced air from the railcar.

He stumbled, his sore paw throwing him off balance. Reach, he commanded his body. He twisted his hips. If he missed—

He stretched his neck to reach just a bit farther. Time seemed to slow as he concentrated on the letter. The railcar, the bag, the clackety-clack, all disappeared. It was just him and the letter. He paddled his paws and opened his mouth as the letter floated free from the bag. He closed his eyes and clamped his teeth, which closed on the envelope. He relaxed his body to land on his feet. He'd done it. Nicole would—

A shock of adrenaline rushed through his body as the speed of the railcar sucked him under the wheels. The train rumbled on as he released his hold on the letter.

Chapter Twenty

Horses pulled carts down the cobblestone streets, their metal shoes echoing off the buildings in the center of the market. Sam scanned the crowd for Stickel and saw him in the distance. He'd turned down an alley just ahead. Market tables covered with fish, baskets, and cheeses, along with all the shoppers blocked her view. The scent of fish and strong cheeses hung in the air as she raced after him.

She stopped at a road and a sign high on a building said "Drury Lane." An empty theater with a marquee void of upcoming shows stood on the corner. Stickel was not in sight, but he'd talked about a theater on Drury Lane. What if he'd established a portal there? Sam shuddered. Which was worse, being in his awful presence or not knowing where he was? She slowed her pace, checking out every door and building, coming across one with white paint on the glass of the windows. She tried to rub it off so she could see inside, but it had been applied to the inside.

She gave an exasperated huff and pushed the door to the theater open. This was the last thing she wanted to do right now, confront Stickel on her own, but Nicole depended on her catching that maniac, and she would be doing all London theater goers a great service besides. No one wanted to see him on the stage, did they?

She ran her finger over a shelf in a row of shelves in

the lobby that ran along a side wall. It hadn't been used for years, and dust covered every surface. The windows at the front of the theater let in filtered light through the white paint. Motes floated in the sunbeams, shining through unpainted windows higher on the wall. Nail holes in the floor created a dotted row showing where a ticket counter had stood. The remnants of brown sugar filled the air, and images of cakes and pies covering the concessions counter had her stomach rumbling.

Her throat tightened and she coughed. She sent up silent thanks to Archie as she pulled out the canteen and took a swig of water. A rustling in the corner made her jump, and she turned as Wilbert pushed himself to all fours, then stood. She held out the canteen, and he tipped his head back and emptied it.

"You look awful." She leveled a glare at him. "Did you see where he went?"

"You mean before he cold cocked me?" He glared back. "You didn't see him race out?"

"No. He must be in the theater somewhere, right?" She scanned the interior. "He is crazy, you know, which makes him unpredictable." She held out a hand to help Wilbert stand. "He's her distant uncle or some such thing."

"You don't say." He grunted as she pulled, and he stood, rubbing the back of his head. "It's more important than ever to find Darlene. He's after her to leverage money from her father. There's no telling how far he'll go." He placed his hat on his head and pulled it down with care. "Her father reported Stickel's recent abuses that have escalated in the last week." Wilbert paced, adding more boot prints to the dusty floor.

Sam rolled her shoulders. Was the temperature here

cooler than outside? This cold seemed supernatural, maybe something to do with the bricks? Where was Archie when she needed him? Wasn't he going to return after he took Nicole home?

Wilbert paced the lobby of the old theater, then stopped in front of her. "Look. Stickel has escaped capture yet again, but he doesn't have Darlene, right? If we hurry, we can be at Darlene's place in under five minutes." Wilbert headed to the door. "I'm more concerned she'll miss her boat tomorrow, at this point, but that could be just what Stickel wants. To keep her family here until he gets the money—"

He raced out the door and took off at a sprint down the street. Sam rushed after him. She couldn't afford to lose him now.

The crowd parted for Wilbert as he charged down the street. She charged past the Bow Street Station, scanning the streets as she jogged. Wilbert skidded around the corner to the right onto Russel that turned into Kemble. She pumped her arms to catch up and glanced down the street at the apartment windows. He stopped on the sidewalk as Darlene and Freddie appeared. She had a rosy blush on her cheeks and her hair stood out in loose, red curls framing her face.

Freddie cradled Darlene's arm in his. What were they still doing in Covent Garden? Shouldn't they be heading to the pier? She glanced at her cell phone. "Gah." How long had she been here? It seemed like a week but was probably only a couple hours.

Wilbert hesitated, a rosy bloom rising to his face. Sam caught up to him, but he ignored her and took a step as a man appeared farther down Kemble. Was that—

Sam gasped. Would Stickel never leave these poor

people alone? "Watch out," she called, but Freddie didn't hear her.

"Father." Darlene choked out, "No," as Stickel hit her father on the back of his head. Freddie crumpled onto the sidewalk. "Father," she cried. "Not again."

Wilbert put his whistle in his mouth and blew. The shrill sound made Sam jump and broke Mr. Stickel's attention. He grabbed Darlene's arm and pulled her down the street. Freddie lay crumpled on the sidewalk.

"Unhand me this instant." Darlene swung her bag.

Mr. Stickel grunted with each blow. Sam couldn't help but grin. Stickel had his hands full. She ran after Wilbert to help Freddie. He was pushing himself from the ground when they reached him.

"My daughter, where is she?" Freddie rose on unsteady legs. He ran his fingers over the lump on the back of his head and growled. "Come on."

He hopped to his feet and took off down Kemble. Wilbert raced after him. Mr. Stickel skidded to the right onto Kean Street. He tugged Darlene, who fought the whole way.

Wilbert blew his whistle again, but Stickel did not slow down.

Freddie halted, breathing hard, and grabbed Wilbert by the shoulders. "Drury Lane. I know where he's going, the theatre. It's a honeycomb of dressing rooms and set construction areas. We must stop him before he gets inside, or we've lost her."

Wilbert kept his gaze on Stickel. They'd have to hurry. "You follow him. I'll backtrack to Drury Lane and stop him before he gets to the theater and tackle him if I must. Sam, you stay here."

Freddie nodded and sprinted down the street after

Stickel. He looked a lot less like Frederick Wilhelm Joseph Meyer III, and more like Freddie with his rumpled and disheveled clothes, but with his stern face and quick reflexes, he was a man on a mission to save his daughter.

Wilbert ran in the opposite direction, another man on a mission for another reason. Did Freddie know how Wilbert felt about his daughter?

Sam clenched her fists. She wasn't staying here and doing nothing. The hair on her arms rose, and she turned toward the market. A tug pulled at her center. Was that her heart or her stomach? Was this the "tug" Nicole was talking about? Before she could stop herself, she was jogging down Great Queen Street.

****

The call of "fresh scones" and "get your fresh cucumbers" rang through the market as Sam reached Floral Street. She turned right onto James Street and found a wooden door to the left unlocked. Whatever was pulling her here wanted her to go underground. The door creaked as she eased it open and followed the stairs into the dim light of the tunnel.

Why here? Did this have something to do with Archie? If not, was it the letter? Why else would she be drawn to this underground tunnel? A white sign with red and black lettering appeared at the bottom of the stairs.

Royal Mail Rail

Covent Garden Market.

Something was wrong. She scanned the shadows where the wall met the floor. Was that a pile of rags?

With her heart in her throat, she raced the distance down the tunnel on winged feet. It was as she feared, an orange tabby.

Archie.

She gasped as she knelt over him. Blood ran from his nostrils and a long gash on his forehead.

"No. You are not dead." Tears ran down her face and into her collar as she pushed her fingers under his furry body. "Oh, Archie." He was still warm. She pulled him into her arms and sat rocking his lifeless form at the side of the tracks.

"No." What had he said about things being fine while there was breath in his body, but he wasn't breathing? What did this mean?

She buried her face in his side and let her tears soak into his fur. She closed her eyes and sobbed. "You were supposed to have two more lives, remember?" She lifted his head. He still had one more, right? Why wasn't he breathing? He couldn't be gone. She ran her hand over his bloody fur. A square of white lay upon the tracks. Was that a letter? Was he killed by the mail rail train?

She buried her face in his fur. "Was the letter more important than your life?" Sam sat and sobbed, holding his body. "Now what do I do?" Her shoulders trembled with her emotion. Was this shock?

A rumbling grew near and brought her to her feet. She held her breath. What was that sound?

The letter. Archie would only put himself in danger for an artifact. She scanned the tunnel and saw the pale, white paper envelope. She laid his body near the wall and turned to the tracks. The clatter was coming fast. She dashed to the letter, pulled it from danger, and backed away to where she'd laid Archie.

Her fingers tingled as she perused the address. It was to Darlene. So, this was how it got lost, a simple untied mail bag? The cars clattered by. They were red and there were only two of them with sacks of mail packed inside both. The tie on one was flapping out a window. Didn't they have anyone monitoring the train?

She turned to Archie. "Was this worth dying for?" A vise-like grip turned her stomach. "Archie?"

Her voice echoed down the empty tunnel as she scurried along the tracks.

****

Wilbert raced after Stickel, and Mr. Meyer huffed and puffed behind him. He was keeping up, but how was Stickel running so fast, the old goat? Wilbert blew his whistle as Stickel skidded to a stop in front of a theater and rushed to a door. Stickel yanked Darlene along behind him. Had he lost her?

Mr. Meyer appeared at the other end of a block, but Mr. Stickel beat them both to a door in an alley that had been left ajar. Darlene opened her mouth to call out, but whatever she said was swallowed as the heavy door swung shut behind her. Wilbert shuddered as the latch locked.

He raced to the door and pulled on the handle. "Locked. Maybe one of the side doors is open." What should he call Darlene's father? Not Frederick or Freddie. No, it would have to be Mr. Meyers. Did he reveal his feelings for this man's daughter? Not now, obviously. His hands shook with the fear of losing Darlene and disappointing her father.

Mr. Meyer winced as he ran his fingers over the lump again. "It's no use. He's gone. This theater is for sale and empty, but it's still a labyrinth of dressing rooms, costume rooms, storage—"

"Got it." Wilbert put a hand on Mr. Meyer's shoulder. "Thank you for your help, sir."

"I would do anything for my daughter." He raked his fingers through his hair. "What is our plan?"

Wilbert nodded. "We have him trapped inside, but he has Darlene. If we don't free her, he'll have a better chance of using her to blackmail you and keep you in London. Is he really an actor?"

"No." Mr. Meyer dropped his chin to his chest. "It seems I've been under his control or running from him all my life. I thought London was the answer, but apparently not."

Wilbert held Mr. Meyer's eye contact. "You were at the final show held in this theater, right? Are you familiar with the layout of this building?"

A fat raindrop landed on Wilbert's cap. Mr. Meyer pulled his coat off and used it to cover his head. "No. All I know is we can't leave her in there for any length of time. He's insane and could hurt her."

"Is there a basement?" Wilbert walked toward the alley behind the theater. "I might have a plan."

"Of course." Mr. Meyer joined him at the corner of the alley. "What are you thinking?"

Wilbert gave a curt nod as he grabbed Mr. Meyer's shoulder and pulled him down the alley at the side of the theater.

Chapter Twenty-One

The tunnel held two sets of tracks, and Sam glanced first right, then left. She reached for Archie, but he was gone. She scratched her head, glancing in both directions. Where did he go? The single lightbulbs that hung from the beams in the ceiling didn't produce enough light for her to make out shapes any distance from the bulb, and the shadows revealed nothing as she jogged down the tunnel. Sam scanned the rounded roof to the point where it met the flat floor, creating shadows. She avoided the tracks. They must be electrified, but was that what killed him?

"Archie." She squinted as she searched.

The strong odor of machine oil stung her eyes. He hadn't been breathing when she found him, so how could he have moved? "Archie." Her voice fell flat in the closed tunnel as another train rattled in the distance.

She patted the letter deep in her shirt and turned back toward the stairs she'd used to enter this underground. A mail railcar rumbled past, and she backed away from the tracks to let it pass. The air current blew particles of dust into the air and her eyes, and she plugged her ears to deaden the clanking of metal wheels on metal tracks.

She pulled her fingers out as the car disappeared around the bend and out of sight, and a movement down the tracks caught her attention. She stared into the distance. There it was again.

"Archie?" She barreled to Archie as he continued dragging himself along the ground. "Archie. You're alive?" He crawled where the roof met the floor, but it provided zero shelter. He cowered there with his head lowered. He didn't have the energy to lift it. She bent down to him, the rust odor of his blood turning her stomach.

Was this the same cat? Is this what happened when he died? He had nine lives, right? What if this had been number nine? They only had twenty-four hours to fix Nicole's family problems, and she still needed him. He was the Protector after all, of the artifacts and bricks and history and magic, and he was growing on her. She wiped a tear from her cheek and put a hand on him, but an electric current jarred her, and she pulled back. "Archie." What was she supposed to do if she couldn't pick him up? Hadn't he said that he had two lives left, which meant now he had one. His body was warm under her palm.

He shook his bloodied head but couldn't speak. His weakness wasn't normal, was it? What was the protocol for a cat returning from the dead? Was she supposed to do something, recite a spell?

She'd stay and watch over him, but how long would this resurrection take? The next train came in fifteen minutes. She squatted on the ground several feet from him. He relaxed visibly, and she closed her eyes.

He mewed, a sound so forlorn it brought tears to her eyes. She'd hated this cat a year ago. She'd found him annoying beyond words and had wished death upon him many times, but she could not stand to see him in this pitiful state. She wanted to pick him up and cradle him, but he'd never allow that, would he? He mewed again.

"Enough." She had to risk his anger. She pulled him into her arms. A current ran through her, and pressure squeezed on her chest.

****

Mr. Meyer jogged down the alley on the left side of the theater. He found a door and pulled it open, stepping inside and stopping. Where would they put the stairs to the basement? Wilbert bungled into his back. Mr. Meyer stumbled and raised a finger to his lips. This kid was going to get them killed with his blundering.

Wilbert nodded and placed a hand on his shoulder. A short hall with multiple doors on each side wasn't confusing at all. If the doors meant rooms, they had almost ten to check. Wilbert pointed to the end of the hall, and Mr. Meyer leaned forward, cupping his ear. Muffled voices came from the main theater.

"You can cry and beg all you want, missy." Mr. Stickel's voice projected throughout the entire theater. Maybe he did have a stage presence. That didn't excuse what he was doing to Darlene.

Mr. Meyer tensed under Wilbert's hand. "Was that a threat? My own cousin? He's getting desperate and might hurt her."

"I have an idea. Where are the steps to the cellar?" Wilbert took a step down the hall. Mr. Meyer followed.

Darlene gave a shriek. "Don't hurt me, Uncle. Father will give you anything you want." Darlene's voice shook, and Mr. Meyer sucked air through his clenched teeth.

Wilbert pushed past Mr. Meyer and tiptoed to the end of the hall. An opening for a stairwell stood on the left. He motioned for Mr. Meyer, and they descended the stairs with care not to make a sound.

"Oh yes, your father will pay." Mr. Stickel laughed. "Let me introduce you to my friend. Mr. George Lawrence."

"Sir." A deep voice filled the air, and Wilbert stopped.

"He brought a goon?" Mr. Meyer turned on the steps, his fists shaking at his side. "Why, I'll—"

"Patience." Wilbert grabbed Mr. Meyer's sleeve. "We just need to get to the boiler. Then we can scare some sense into this fiend."

Mr. Meyer hesitated, before giving a nod. Wilbert raced down the last couple stairs and into a vast dark space. Several wooden crates sat against the wall to the right. Light seeped in through a dirty window to the left and high in the wall, and the heavy odor of coal dust filled the place. A candle and a box of matches sat on the windowsill.

Wilbert handed the candle to Mr. Meyer and lit a match, holding it to the wick. Mr. Meyer held the candle up and walked to the center of the cellar, illuminating the cavernous space.

"There." Mr. Meyer pointed. A coal bin with a chute running to street level slanted into a large wooden bin. Opposite the bin was a boiler.

Wilbert nudged Mr. Meyer. "What say we have some fun with this madman?"

****

The scent of lavender filled Sam's nostrils as she fell onto her side, cradling Archie. The thick padding under the familiar wool rug pattern made a soft place to land. Dad's jaw dropped, and she would have laughed, but the sight of Nicole sitting beside him stopped her. Nicole's pale face and drooping eyes stopped Sam. Who needed help more, her or Archie?

Sam lifted Archie's limp body and, pressing her eyes closed, rocked him gently in her arms. Dad rose, his mouth open to speak but no sound came out.

"Dad, he was dead, but—" Sam's vision blurred as she held Archie to her chest, rocking him. She stopped as he pushed with his bloodied paw, and she set him on a footstool with a folded blanket covering it. He sprawled out on his side, panting.

Dad joined Sam on the floor.

She swiped at her tear-stained eyes. "But he's alive now. He's got a cut on his forehead that might need stitches, and blood is drying on a gash on his side."

"I'll clean him up while you tell me everything." Dad had a packet of antiseptic wipes and started on Archie's nose. "Did you see what happened?" He placed a hand on Archie's side as he used a wipe to clean up the blood.

"No." Sam winced. "I thought he was an old rag at first, but I recognized the color of his fur." She shook her head. She'd never get that image from her mind.

"Did you check for broken bones?" Dad threw the bloody wipes in a wastebasket by the table. Archie lay unmoving on his side, his ribs rising and falling.

Sam shook her head. "Is that part of the training you should be giving me?" She tugged on her ear. "I had no idea what to do, so I picked him up, and next thing I knew, we'd jumped here without a second's warning."

Dad ran his hands down each of Archie's legs and over his ribs. "Nothing seems broken." Archie mewed, and Dad patted his shoulder. "Where did you find him?"

"In the Royal Mail Rail tunnel and I found this lying

near his body." She held up the letter and the hair raised from her wrist to her elbow. She dropped it, and Dad pulled her into a hug. She let herself sob into his shoulder. "I have never felt so helpless. I am not a nurse, Dad." She pulled away, and he wiped a tear from her cheek with his thumb before it reached her chin. All her anger and frustration at his unwillingness to teach her disappeared in that moment.

"You did everything right, apparently." He shot her a quick smile.

"What does that mean?" Sam wiped a trembling hand across her forehead.

"Archie needed your tears. It's what revived him." Dad peered into her eyes.

"My tears? I still have so much to learn." She backed away and punched her fist against her thigh.

"Each case is so different and unique, there is no way to guess what knowledge you will need in any given situation." He bit his lip.

She nodded. That made sense in a weird-logic sort of way. "So, you think Archie will be okay?"

"I'm sure of it." Dad rested his hand on the footstool next to the cat.

His caution not to disturb Archie did not escape her notice. Dad was worried that he was still weak.

She wanted to believe what he was telling her, but he seemed so distracted and lost sometimes when she was involved with the magic. She glanced at Archie, who cleaned up better than she'd imagined. She stood and moved to the couch. "And what's going on with Nicole?"

"Nicole is sitting right here, thanks." She scowled at Sam.

"Sassy. That's a good sign." Sam's stomach tied in

a knot.

Nicole's face was too pale, like her blood had been drained from her body. She didn't lift a finger to stop Sam as she lifted Nicole's hair from her face and tucked it behind her ear. Did she have the energy to raise her arm even?

"Nicole's helping me locate her mom, right?" Dad smiled at Nicole.

"She wasn't in the house when I rushed over here with that letter. Was that just yesterday?" Nicole shifted her body on the couch and coughed. "I didn't realize she was involved, but her name—"

"Dad—" Sam glared at him, but he focused on Nicole.

"We'll find her, but we need Archie's help." Dad rose and pulled open the vault door. He rummaged through the vials in the cabinet with clinks and clatters. "Archie needs a tonic. Can you run to the kitchen and bring me a bowl of milk, Sam?"

Was he trying to keep her occupied? Sam raised a hand to her friend, but let it drop to her side. Archie, Nicole, and Mrs. Blevins? She stood. Nicole was running on borrowed time, and they needed Archie if they were going to help her.

Sam dipped her chin. "Sure." She headed to the stairs.

"One of Archie's bowls, not Mom's good china," Dad called after her as she plodded up the stairs.

Mom considered him more animal than human, so made sure he used his own plates and glasses even when he was in human form. It had never caught her attention before, but geez. Now it seemed so obvious and a form of speciesism.

The hallway to the entry had never seemed so long as it did right now. She yawned. Was it jetlag? Or jump-lag? She walked across the star on the entry floor and turned right down another hall that had an open wall to the living room, then the dining room.

Since the funeral, it was as if her life belonged to someone else. Her parents kept saying they weren't rich, but really? The chandeliers hanging in the living and dining room glittered and cast rainbows from the crystal prisms dangling from polished brass fixtures.

She opened the fridge and grabbed the quart of milk and Archie's favorite cobalt blue bowl. She retraced her steps and handed the bowl to Dad. He sat on the footstool with Archie in his lap.

"Pour out about a cup of milk, will you. Then add the contents of this vial over the milk. Don't touch it, whatever you do."

"Why?"

"You don't want to know. Suffice it to say, this will restore Archie to better feline health. Even so, it will be a while before he'll be able to change to human form or jump through time, so—"

Sam glared at Dad. "Jump? You think he's going to jump any time soon? Not after dying. None of us are going to jump."

"Now hold on." Dad frowned at her. "We don't have a choice or time to argue, I'm afraid. Archie jumped because Uncle Charles has Darlene in his custody, and things are critical. Just look at Nicole. Her weakness is the effect of his meddling." Dad pressed his lips together, and Sam tensed. He only did that when he was worried. "We might have to jump within the hour."

Sam backed away from him, shaking her head.

"No—"

"Sam," Nicole called her from the couch. "I need to save Mom. I have to go with you."

Sam glared at Dad. "Now look what you've done. Nicole can't jump. Not in her condition."

"London and Darlene hold the key to this debacle. Another jump may be the only thing that saves Nicole and her mother."

Sam sank onto the floor next to the footstool. "Oh, Dad. We need Archie, but how will he be ready in time?" She sobbed into her hands.

"Coming back from the dead is never easy, but he will recover." Dad pulled her to stand and wrapped her in his arms, his deep voice rumbling in his chest. "Then we can help Nicole save her family."

A groan from the stool stopped her, and she gasped. Archie lifted his head, his eyes mere slits in his furry face.

"Sam—prepare—to learn." He dropped his head and lay still as death.

Sam shuddered. "What?"

"He's not dying, Sam. You still have much to learn, and Nicole needs your help." He shook his head and moved to the stairs. "I'm going to talk to Mom. We'll be leaving soon."

Sam stared at the footstool. Strong? She glanced at Archie on his stool, but his vulnerable state melted her heart.

"Okay. I'm ready for the next lesson, but will you be?"

Archie didn't move, but a grin formed on his feline lips.

Chapter Twenty-Two

The family Bible and *The Tome of Truth,* along with maps of London and Covent Garden, lay sprawled over the mahogany table. Dad leaned over the Bible. This is exactly what Archie had her do, and once she had touched the names and words, they were part of her memory.

Dad whispered to himself as he pressed his finger over the names of a tree. What was he up to? Sam squirmed as she held Nicole's hand while she slept. Archie wasn't much better. Sam bobbed her knee, and she clamped her eyes shut. Nicole's cheeks were pale, and Archie hadn't moved since he'd drunk the potion. Was this normal in the magical world of artifacts, Guardians, and Protectors?

She opened her eyes to slits. Archie's tail had a bend near the tip that hadn't been there before. He was lucky he hadn't broken every bone in his body. His girth was rounder, so he must be healing, but why did the potion have to take so long?

"I hate just sitting around and doing nothing." Sam crossed her arms over her midriff.

Dad cringed. "We're not doing nothing." He raised his head and gave her a lopsided grin. "Get it? Not doing nothing? It's a double negative, so we are doing something."

"Dad. Quit with the double negatives." She shot him

her best stink eye, which caused a sharp pain to shoot through her head.

Dad cleared his throat and gave her a curt nod. "It's all here in the *Tome*—"

She held up a hand. "Really? Is this part of my lessons?"

Dad grabbed Sam's hand. "I don't like it either, but we don't have Archie to guide us, do we?" He pointed to a spot on a page. "Read this."

She rose and stepped closer to the table. She pushed maps and other documents out of the way and pulled *The Tome* closer. What was happening with Wilbert and Freddie? Had they rescued Darlene? Hopefully, Wilbert had apprehended Stickel, that lunatic.

"Please explain." She stared at the words written in something other than English.

Dad pulled the book closer and read. "The names will be restored if the time continuum can be restored. Each case will be unique, so these instructions are general and must be interpreted by the Guardian with the Protector, but there will be markers to lead the Guardian to the source of the disruption."

Sam raked her fingers through her head. "Is that supposed to be helpful?"

Nicole sneezed, and Sam rushed to her side. Thank all the goddesses she was waking up. Nicole mumbled something unintelligible and settled into the blankets on the couch without opening her eyes.

Sam placed a hand to Nicole's forehead. "Her temperature is normal. That's good, right?"

Dad nodded and pointed to the page, but Sam stood over Nicole, not wanting to break the contact with her. What would she do without Nicole? She shuddered.

Don't go there.

She returned to the table and returned her finger to the place where Dad had left off. "This madness begins and ends with Darlene, but what is the solution?"

Dad didn't respond. He kept his finger on the page.

"Why didn't the bricks come with a manual, so we could just look up what we need to do?"

Dad leaned against the huge table. He turned to her. "*The Tome* is our manual."

His forehead wrinkles were going to be permanent if they didn't catch Stickel soon. Nicole snorted in her sleep from the couch, and Dad reached behind him to pull a blanket up around her shoulders.

Sam gazed at the page again. "Dad, how could you read this?"

"Let's just say being the Guardian means some serious upgrades, like fluency in the language of the Tome." He shrugged.

She scoffed. "A dad-joke, really?" She turned to skim the page. The letters and accents went from random symbols to formed words, and soon they made sense to her. She began reading as fast as she could.

****

The streetlamps blinked on, shining a golden light through the colorful windows of the throne room. Sam rested on her palms as she turned to Dad. "So, did you know that Archie would die, and you'd have to make that potion? Did Archie know?"

"I had no idea, but Archie had guessed."

"How? Can he predict the future?"

"No. It's like Archie says, 'magic is not an exact science.' But he must put himself in danger if the situation calls for it. Plus, we're dealing with what

Stickel does at any given time, and considering the man's insane—"

"So, you know he's bat-sh—"

"Language." Dad frowned at her. "But as the Protector of—"

"Protector, I know, Dad, but—" She squinted at Dad. "Does that make Archie an artifact?"

"I never thought of that before. He came into being the same time as the bricks, but I don't know." He shrugged. "Archie protects the artifacts, and he's just died, so maybe not?"

Sam pressed her hands to her temples. "My head hurts. It was awful finding him like that—"

She ran her fingers over her trembling lips. "How many more lives does he have, and what does he do when the last one ends? Does he have an heir, and would it be a kitten?" She placed a hand to her head as if to support the weight of it.

Dad placed his hand on her shoulder. It was large and warm and calmed her. "I know, it's a lot to take in. He and Aunt Eli regularly kept track of his offspring, just in case. He knows of a recent litter where one kitten shows promise."

"What does that mean? Can it talk? Has it shifted to human form a couple times?" She threw her hands in the air. "No wonder Mom can't handle this. This is too random for her logical brain, isn't it?"

"Yes, it is." Dad shrugged. "Who knows how long it will take him to train the next Protector."

Archie mewed from the floor. Sam rushed to his side. The stitches on his forehead wiggled as he tried to move, and his fur was dull where it wasn't covered in blood and grime. His breathing was deeper, though. She pulled a throw blanket from the throne and covered him with it. She tucked in the edges and stood with a sigh.

Dad shoved his hands in his pockets. "He is crucial in solving this London problem with Mr. Stickel."

"Oh—my—goddess. If I hear his name one more time."

Nicole pushed up on an elbow. "What name?"

Sam turned to the couch. "You're awake? Finally, there is some color in your cheeks again." She let her shoulders slump with a sigh.

"I feel stronger suddenly. Did you give me something?" Nicole swung her legs onto the floor and patted her curls.

Dad shook his head. "There's only one cure for your malady. Stickel must be stopped. You'll need your strength, as will Archie, because what comes next will tax us all."

Dad stood and jogged up the stairs.

Sam took Nicole's hand as a shudder shook Nicole's body.

Chapter Twenty-Three

The maroon drapes of the throne room came into focus as Archie cracked open an eyelid. He inhaled and exhaled as if he'd forgotten how, his lungs burning with each breath. Wisps of lavender tickled his nostrils, and he sighed.

Home. How had he gotten here?

He blinked. Sam, of course. Bless that child. He lifted his head, but a wave of dizziness hit, and he sank onto the pillow. Why did everything have to hurt? All his years wore him down. Since 377 BC to this day, subtract seven—

No. It was eight. He had lost eight lives. That would make it 2400 years, give or take. He was an old geezer, as Sam would say. He chuckled and gasped. No wonder he was sore.

He tried to open both his eyelids, but they refused to budge. The healing process had varied with each death. He shuddered. He'd been out for weeks with previous regenerations, and he lost a life every time. His tail throbbed, just like that time in Athens, Greece. He hadn't died, but he'd wished he had until it healed. He couldn't inhale without a stabbing pain in his lungs.

P-A-T-H-E-T-I-C.

He tried to lick his sore paw, but his body spasmed. Note to Archie: no bathing.

He could still think, so he'd use this time to think

about an heir. He had had a litter with the striking Isabelle from two blocks down.

Belle.

In the past one thousand years, he hadn't met another feline like her. One of the little gingers in the litter reminded him of himself as a young kit. He wiggled an eyebrow. It didn't hurt.

He grinned. It was almost time to wean the kits. Perfect. He'd have a living reminder of Belle for the rest of his life. Bella.

He was always impatient to heal. Sam and Nicole needed him, or did they? They needed a Protector of the Artifacts. That was certain.

He curled tighter in a ball. He had an heir to acknowledge and indoctrinate with the *Scintilla Vitae,* the spark of life.

He gritted his teeth. He would only have one chance at this. He peered from the slits of his eyelids. Was that Nicole? Bundled under a tussle of blankets, curled on the couch? They were a fine pair. He clamped his eyes shut and settled on the footstool, its familiar contours easing the tension from his shoulders and hips. He purred, and his chest fluttered. If only his ninth life would be long.

A child. My child.

He closed his eyes and tucked his head into his body. He would enjoy training Sam beside his son.

****

The stained-glass windows cast their patterns onto the mahogany table as sunshine filtered through them. She measured time by meals, and it must be lunchtime by the sound of her tummy rumblings.

The serene effect of the throne room did nothing to

distract Sam from her angst as she gripped the edge of the couch cushion. Archie leaned against the table in human form, and she cringed.

How many times had she sat right here and watched as Aunt Eli poured over the *Tome of Truth* with no idea what the book was? She loved the purple velvet cover and the mystery surrounding the book. But now?

Why had Aunt Eli died now? Was it her death that had left Nicole's family vulnerable? Sam glanced at Archie as he gripped the edge of the table for support. He seemed so unkempt and frail in his baggy suit pants, his shirt untucked in the front, his vest unbuttoned. Her throat constricted. He hadn't recovered yet.

He turned to gaze at her with his unblinking amber eyes. She lowered her eyes.

Was he a mind reader, too?

"This lesson comes after you need it, I'm afraid." He coughed and pressed a hand to his chest.

"Archie, you're not strong enough." She reached out a hand to him. Why hadn't he stayed in cat form? "You're too weak—"

He held up a hand. "The mistress wanted to wait until we were certain before telling you, but I am quite certain now." He cleared his throat and hesitated.

"Tell me what? What's happening?" Sunlight slanted through the stained glass, and she squinted. Archie hunched over, a silhouette against the bright backlighting from the windows.

He coughed. "It has rarely happened this way before. For almost two thousand years, the bricks have passed from one generation to the next, so I expected your father to be—"

"Helping me, right? That's what you were going to

say." She jumped to her feet.

Archie put a hand to the stitches on his head. "No. He should be doing it all. You shouldn't even be involved. He should be the next Guardian, but you—"

"I what?" She blinked and waited.

Archie heaved a sigh that shook his entire frame. "Do you remember the Old Pioneers Underground Tour?" He folded his arms over his chest.

"Yes—" She stood and paced to the fireplace and back to the couch. "Wait. Is this about Portland?"

Archie lowered his chin to his chest. "James took the lead on that mission. It was his first, but you interrupted the flow of magic by using the bricks before he had stopped Stickel." Archie stared at Aunt Eli's throne as if she sat there and he was addressing her. "We should have started James' training long before we did, but the mistress had concerns. James couldn't convince Carol of the importance of—"

"Wait? What are you saying?" The sound of her pulse pounded in her ears.

Archie hung his head. "The Guardian needs a spouse who supports the mission to protect and guard the artifacts."

"But he didn't tell her?"

"She wouldn't listen."

"And she kicked him out when he tried." Sam put a hand to her cheek. "That's why he left last year. That's what caused me to touch those bricks." She paced the floor in front of the table. "I thought they were headed for a divorce over that note, the lavender scent." She stopped and raised a hand to her head. "I just wanted Dad back."

Archie nodded. "But now you know how and why

the bricks work, and even though you accomplished your goal, so much has been affected and changed."

Archie lowered himself to perch on the footstool. "Aunt Eli was too weak with vertigo to stop Stickel. We had to rely on James who—"

"Wasn't ready." Sam pressed her lips together. This new understanding caused a tightness in her chest. He'd said he would return soon. Why did she think she could fix it?

"So, it was his first mission?" Sam leaned against the table. "He must have been as confused as I was." And she'd thought he knew everything. Poor Dad.

"Mistress Eli and I had been working with him, but Charles found a way to activate the bricks in Portland by using Freddie and Elise, which set off the chain of events—"

Sam gripped the table with her fingers. "And Nicole. She was able to use them too because—"

"You are related." Archie's eyes sagged at the corners, but he held eye contact. "You are cousins. You know that now, and I think you understand what I'm going to say next." He stared at her, and she held her breath. "The bricks should have chosen James as the next Guardian, but his love for you will always override his duty to any mission. You, on the other hand, have focused on solving any problem without the same emotional distractions. Mistress Eli was never prouder of you than when you sorted the Portland dilemma."

"It wasn't just me."

Archie held up a hand. "That is the other reason the bricks are choosing you. You do not use the bricks for your own gain, and you would never hurt another person. We don't know what your father would do to Stickel—"

"You mean—"

Archie nodded.

She stared at the colorful geometric patterns cast on the floor and across the table. "He didn't kill him, though."

"No, but he will never be able to fully focus on any mission if you are involved, and Carol's fears will never allow her to accept or support him as Guardian."

Sam shoved her hands in her pockets. She could relate. The bricks and all the artifacts were complicated in a way that should frighten anyone involved with them. "But I don't need her support?"

"Your relationship is different."

Sam shook her head. "So, you were right? The bricks chose me over Dad? Does that mean I'm the next—"

"Guardian of the artifacts, yes." Archie pushed himself to a stand but stumbled.

"Whoa. You're exhausted. You need to rest—"

She took his arm and helped him settle in the throne. A fire crackled in the fireplace, and the aroma of cedar smoke filled her senses.

He took her hand from his arm and patted it. "I'm fine. I'm just glad that you finally understand the truth. I wish I could have told you this earlier."

She sank on the couch beside him. Archie's hands shook. It had taken all his strength to deliver that lesson, but he hadn't quit until she fully comprehended him. He'd never meant her harm. He was only trying to protect the family and the artifacts. A wave of warmth filled her chest. "So, what happens now?"

"I have a *Glemme* potion for your mom and your dad when the time is right. We still need his help. For now, we'll focus on Nicole."

He patted her hand and closed his eyes, slipping into cat form and leaving a pile of clothes on the throne. She lifted him and placed him gently on the footstool, as Mom called to her, "Lunch is ready."

She turned to take one last glance at Nicole. She couldn't wait to tell her she trusted Archie.

Chapter Twenty-Four

A moan rose from the couch, and Nicole realized it came from her. All she did was sleep, but that's all she could do. Time travel left her fully drained, and whatever Stickel was doing sucked her energy further. The throne room seemed unchanged, but she was—

What was she? Different somehow.

Archie glanced at her. "You're awake. Are you hungry?"

She slipped off the blanket, stood, and stretched. "What happened to you?"

"I died."

"Is that your attempt at humor? You look like Frankenstein."

Archie cocked an eyebrow at her without otherwise changing his expression. "Are you hungry or not?"

"I could eat. I'm sorry you died."

He swatted the air as if brushing away an annoyance.

She shook her head. "Where's Sam?"

"In the kitchen. Carol made lunch." Archie walked to her.

The knot in Nicole's stomach tightened as she sat on the edge of the couch. "If we are both healed, this means a trip to 1929 is inevitable." The thought of traveling through time made her knees weak.

He forced a grin, and Nicole saw the pain in his eyes.

Did he have bad news? He must because that was the I-have-bad-news look.

Archie focused his unblinking eyes on her. "As you know, you have the family blood."

Nicole kept her gaze on the carpet. "So—does this change anything, or everything?"

"It changes some things, but not everything, and that has complicated our usual approach to making adjustments."

"What does that even mean?" She clasped her hands together and laid them in her lap.

"Have you heard the term 'adjustment'? It's the best word to describe what we do. We must adjust the negative energy by stopping people who would use the bricks for their own gain, in this case, Mr. Stickel, from coercing money from Freddie for his profit. It might seem a bit backward and counterintuitive, but if we jump back and stop Stickel, we can adjust history to match the present. It has worked for us over the millennia."

"Don't you mean millennium?"

"Millennia is the plural form of millennium, which means a thousand years, but you knew that. Two thousand years plus far surpasses a millennium." Archie waved his hand through the air with a dismissive flair.

She shook her head. Did he just fact-shame her? "But what do millennia have to do with me?"

"Mr. Stickel's actions are once again causing a rift in the time-space continuum, which affects the negative energy—"

She swatted the air with her limp hand. "You've already explained that. How is that even helpful?"

Archie cocked his eyebrow and winced. "You must go back with Sam. If Darlene stands a chance of being rescued, it will take all of us and the letter she apparently never received." He strode to the table and placed a hand on the *Tome* and a map. "Using this map I've drawn, you will find Stickel, Darlene, Freddie, and Wilbert in this empty theater. It's huge and it's dark. I'll need your help in devising a plan, while I work from here."

"But when?"

"Now." He heaved a heavy breath. "We need Sam's help, too."

Sam trotted down the final steps to the room, balancing a plate of sandwiches on her arm. She skidded to a stop. "What?"

Archie took a sandwich. "We must plan your next step, then eat and run, as they say."

****

The curtains to the vault swished as Archie pulled them aside to reveal the bricks. Nicole peered into the vault as she clutched Sam's hand. Archie gave the letter to Nicole and squeezed her hand. Nicole gave a faint nod.

He clasped his hands as if in prayer. "I died for this. Please, don't lose it."

He returned to lean against the massive mahogany table, its carvings deep and filled with shadows. The bank of windows on the south wall reflected the interior lights. Why had he changed to human form if he wasn't going with them? Wasn't he fully healed?

Sam's smile didn't reach her eyes. Nicole wasn't brave enough to smile. Could she do this? Was she strong enough? Did they have a choice? She was exhausted, but the one thing they didn't have was time, for a nap, to heal, to make a solid working plan.

She gripped her hands into fists to stop them from shaking. She had to get to the theater. Would Freddie and

Wilbert be there? She hoped so because she and Sam were going to need all the help they could get. Could Nicole even find the theater again? A sense of calm filled her.

"It's time to go." Sam held her hand out, and Nicole put hers over it. She gave Sam the letter, and she tucked it in her coat pocket, then pressed her hand onto the bricks. The pressure on Nicole's chest squeezed all the air from her lungs.

****

Wilbert put his hand on a pipe that ran from the boiler to the ceiling and alongside a beam. "It's hot. It leads to a radiator in the theater, but which one?"

"Just hit it, and we'll find out soon enough." Mr. Meyer moved closer.

Wilbert put a hand to his ear. He could make out mumbles, but not words, as Mr. Stickel harangued Darlene. He glanced at Mr. Meyer. Should he reveal that he was going to America on the same ship? No. Could he trust Darlene's father not to murder Mr. Stickel when they found him? Also no. He picked up a short plank of wood and hit the pipe.

The mumbling stopped. Mr. Meyer opened the door to the boiler with a slow screech. Coal embers still glowed red from within the metal furnace. The heavy stench of it burnt his nostrils. He coughed, then yelled into the belly of the furnace. "Chaaarrrrllleessss?"

Footsteps sounded on the floor above.

"He's running." Mr. Meyer shut the boiler door and turned to face the stairs.

Mr. Stickel appeared holding a lantern. Light flooded the cellar and the boiler. "Well. Look what the cat dragged in." He shook his finger at Mr. Meyer.

"Wha—"

"Don't look so surprised? Do you think this is the first time someone has tried the ghosts-through-the-boiler routine on me? You fool." Mr. Stickel shook his head at Mr. Meyer, then tipped his head back in laughter.

The hair rose on the back of Wilbert's neck. "Where is Darlene?" He stabbed a finger at Stickel. "If anything has happened to her…"

Stickel grinned. "Just you never mind." He turned his attention to Mr. Meyer.

Wilbert wracked his brain for a diversion. He scanned the walls and floor, something to use as a weapon.

Stickel's cackle stopped him cold. The man was insane.

"You are trying to cheat me out of my money, but that isn't going to happen. Now, here's what you are going to do."

Wilbert waved his arm, drawing Stickel's attention. He took a step forward as Mr. Meyer made a dash for the stairs, but Stickel knocked him to the ground. Wilbert stopped, transfixed. Stickel's eyes focused on Mr. Meyer. He was far more dangerous than anyone Wilbert had ever encountered before. With his sagging jowls and his clothes hanging off his sparse frame, he had surprising quickness and strength.

Wilbert tripped and sprawled on the cement floor as Mr. Stickel threw his lantern in the coal bin and stood a grin splitting his sweaty face. An explosion filled the basement, and flames lit up the wooden walls of the bin.

"Mr. Meyer!" Wilbert called, but Mr. Meyer had raced after Stickel.

Mr. Stickel pulled the door closed, and Wilbert's

stomach knotted as the lock latched.

Mr. Meyer pounded on the door to no avail. Wilbert had to stand, but his arms were like rubber. He choked out a cough. Mr. Meyer pressed a kerchief over his mouth against the smoke billowing from the growing fire.

"We're trapped."

Chapter Twenty-Five

Light shone through the kitchen window and onto the black and white tiles of the kitchen floor. James stroked Carol's cheek, but she averted her eyes. They sat across from one another, and he could sense the shift in her attitude toward the magic she had opposed for so long.

"I need to be involved. I can trust you, but not that cat. I need to help you watch my daughter." She'd crossed her arms over her chest.

A sense of calm settled in his chest. He'd dreamed of Carol's acceptance for so long. Becoming the Guardian was hard enough, but now that it had become clear that Sam would be the next Guardian and not him, he needed Carol's help more than ever.

He sat silent. What could he say? What words of encouragement would console this intelligent, beautiful woman? He blurted, "I don't—"

She held up a hand. "Let me speak." She stared at her folded hands on the table. "I can no longer avoid the magic." She pushed back the chair and stood. "I can't wallow in fear. I mean, I'm terrified, don't get me wrong, but Sam must time-travel and use the artifacts to maintain some sort of balance, right? That has become crystal clear to me, and who's going to keep her safe as she puts her life in danger? You? Archie?"

She dropped her head in her hands, then wiped her

eyes and cleared her throat. "I must be involved." She gave him a small nod.

He put a hand to his heart. Her tiny frame held a fierce mother's heart. She would become the Grandma Meyer of her generation. The matriarch of the family. She wouldn't have the ability to use the magic, but she would know and understand it and keep the knowledge safe and alive.

He let his hand drop to his side. "I can't tell you—"

"I know, James, but tell me what I need to do. I need to help." Her eyes held his until his vision blurred.

He'd waited for her to join him in this magical realm, and here she was. He stood and searched the kitchen walls and ceiling. Where did he begin? With the present. He walked to her side. "Archie and Nicole are recovering, so we'll be jumping to the past soon."

"Jumping?" She tilted her head, her mouth pinched but her eyes bright.

This was her trying. He nodded. "That's what we call time travel, jumping or leaping through time." He pulled her to her feet. "I'll lay out some books on the table in the throne room, and you can start reading." He draped his arm over her shoulder as they walked to the front door.

"I can do that. Knowledge is power, right? You better be careful." She had the look of the literature professor she was, as she lifted her book bag and her purse from the floor by the door. She had to deliver a lecture on E.M. Forrester at the university. How many times had they stood on this star in the last two months saying their goodbyes, but this time was different. They both had a role to play in this magical journey.

He kissed her brow. "I'll see you this afternoon."

She gave a curt nod and shrugged into her raincoat, slipping out the front door, trotting down the steps. He stood on the porch until she'd disappeared behind the neighbor's hedge.

He closed the door and leaned against it. Would this bring them closer together or tear them apart?

****

James jogged down the stairs. How would Archie take Carol's news? As Protector, had he sensed her acquiescence?

Archie lifted his head and gave him a nod before returning to his nap. This was really happening, and James couldn't stop the wave of fear that rolled through his chest. Archie had died. Was it because Aunt Eli had not finished preparing him to be the next Guardian? Was there way any way to prepare for the death of the Protector? Or to protect Carol from the dangers that she might not understand?

He shook his head. No therapist on the planet could help him through this, a magical cat who died and came back to life? They'd lock him up and throw away the key.

He crossed his arms and scowled at the vault. The scent of lavender and bleach hung heavy in the air, which meant Sam had jumped to London with Nicole. He tightened his fists to stop his hands from shaking. Nicole using the artifacts was unprecedented. How did that even happen?

Archie sneezed in his sleep and cracked open an eyelid and sat in the middle of the blanket on his footstool, waiting as if he knew what James would say.

James leaned on the edge of the table. "Carol's decided to help. She wants to know more about this world her daughter is being drawn into, so you'll have another pupil. Sam needs all the support we can give her, especially from her mother, as she learns to be the Guardian."

Archie stared at him. Was he going to disagree? He'd wanted to dose her with that bitter memory-wiping tea.

Why didn't Archie say something? He scowled at the cat. "Carol could be our very own 'Grandma Meyer.' The family member who researches the artifacts in the throne room and keeps the knowledge of the *Tome* alive. If we don't approach the magic of the artifacts and time travel as a family, we'll never succeed." James took a steadying breath. How did he say this next part? "Besides, this is—"

Archie raised an eyebrow, which in his cat-form was disarming to say the least. "My last life. I am aware." Archie's voice rasped like coarse sandpaper on rough wood. "I found the moment of infinitum. Do you know what that is? That moment when all outcomes are possible. Like Schrodinger's cat."

James started. He closed his eyes, searching his brain for the theory of Schrodinger's cat, and it emerged. That a cat in a box meant multiple possibilities existed until the box was opened: death, life, failure, success. How apropos.

Stretching his back and yawning, Archie jumped from the stool. "I watched those mail railcars rattle by, knowing if that letter was lost, we would never save Nicole. Her family would have ended with Darlene."

James shook his head. "I'm still confused by Wilbert's involvement. Wasn't Darlene engaged to Graham when Nicole arrived?"

"Nicole jumped at the same time Graham's name

was disappearing. With Graham's decision not to immigrate to America, Darlene could not stay engaged, which means she wasn't very serious about him."

James frowned. "So we were on the wrong—"

He couldn't finish his statement. Archie in cat-form had never seemed smaller to James, nor more vulnerable. Archie leaned against the footstool, pulling the blanket onto the floor and stepping into the pile of soft cloth.

"I just sensed the power of that letter as it floated out of the mailbag, as if I didn't try to catch it, Nicole's bloodline would perish, and everything Sam had done up to this point would have been for naught. Then, there is the matter of my fondness for Miss Blevins." He wiped his nose on the blanket.

James perused the contents of the large table: maps, scrolls, books. A warm sense of relief filled him that Carol was willing to help sort through this family history. She'd support Sam, affirming her success on this and future missions. "Well then, my friend." He gave Archie a small smile. "We have a lot of work to do."

****

James touched the velvet curtain that covered the bricks. They had been activated, and no one could stop what happened next. Could he protect Sam? She'd been through so much, and as much as he'd wanted to save her from danger, she'd proven herself to be more than capable. She was more adept at being the Guardian as a teenager than he'd been at thirty when Aunt Eli first started his training.

Archie jumped from the footstool. His ragged appearance made James' entire body ache with sympathy. With only one life left, that meant—

Archie coughed and sat on his haunches. "I need my

heir."

"He is weaned and ready to join us, but should you be talking in cat-form? Your lungs—"

"I need—"

"I heard you the first time. I've talked to Mrs. Patterson, and she's waiting for my arrival, but without Aunt Eli—"

"Don't remind me." Archie twitched his shoulder. "Mistress Eli has saved many a kitten in her time. If only she—"

"I have all the contact information of potential owners. She left them in the vault, so the rest of your offspring will have only the best homes."

"They don't only need the 'best.' They also need the 'right' homes." Archie coughed.

James held up his hands. "Don't upset yourself, my old friend. I've taken all the precautions, and the right home for each kitten will reveal itself."

"They are all potential heirs."

"I know." James lifted Archie into his arms. In his cat-form, he was light as a feather. Archie pushed against his chest. He hated being held. "I'm glad you're feeling better, but I'd like to carry you up the stairs at least. We can't lose you before we've performed the ceremony."

"I've thought of a name." Archie settled in James' arms. "Leonardo."

"That's a good name, Archie, a strong name." James patted Archie's head, and Archie bit at his fingers. James chuckled. He knew better than to pet a magic cat. They climbed the rest of the stairs in silence.

Chapter Twenty-Six

The kitten had slept on the car ride home. Granted it was only ten blocks, but with all the traffic signals and starts and stops, was that normal? This might just be the ticket to Archie's recovery. James carried the kitten into the house. It fit in the palm of his hand, and James' chest constricted as he carried the tiny animal down the marble staircase to the throne room. What kind of life lay in store for this little guy?

James stopped on the last step. How did Archie get downstairs? He stood in human form, dressed in his ceremonial robe of purple velvet with a jeweled scepter in his right hand. It was tipped with a smooth, golden globe, and James pulled the kitten tighter as he slept in his arms. Aunt Eli had warned him of this ceremony, but the reality of the opulence was a shock. The gold brocade on the cloak alone must weigh—

"Are you strong enough for this?"

"I have no choice. Sam and Nicole could need us at any minute, but I must decree my heir's name before the Universe and the artifacts before I jump to the past and perhaps depart this mortal coil."

That was bit dramatic, but James nodded. "Where does Little-Leo go?"

Archie chuckled. "He is a bit of scruff, isn't he? My son. My heir. He will sleep through most of this, I hope. Place him on the blanket that I've arranged on this footstool." He motioned to a fuzzy blanket on the footstool that Archie had somehow moved to the vault under the bricks. The maroon, velvet curtains lent it a royal flair.

James laid the kitten on the footstool and backed away. The kitten didn't stir. He was so tiny. James glanced at Archie.

A tear ran down Archie's face. "I never wanted this life, I had no idea it even existed, but now that I have lived it, and I have learned my way between two worlds, human and feline, I am bound to bestow it upon an heir, you, my natural born son.

"I have mastered my way through the magic of the bricks and the blood-magic. I am proud to be the Protector of these artifacts." Archie cleared his throat and continued.

He bowed over the table and stared at the words from a leather-bound book. "I consecrate this space for the naming ritual, *An Deas-Ghnath Ainmeahaidh*." He wiped his brow, and James took a step forward. Archie shot him a look, and James stepped back.

"I will begin with the legend of the Names. I proclaim these words as true: My first name was *Buna Asta*, Wise One, a silly name given me by a leader of men, Guillem the Wise, who loved me as much as I loved him. I would have saved his life if I could have." Archie coughed. James took a step closer, but Archie waved him away.

Archie continued in a stronger voice. "When the Romans slaughtered my master, I became the shadow cat, *Pisica de Umbra*. I lived in the dark place and took solace in the tears of my master's wife, Beda. Her tears on my fur brought me peace. When she died, her oldest son, Brogdon, renamed me *Pisica Caramizilor,* Cat of the Bricks. My first death was at his hand. He blamed me for his mother's constant grief, and perhaps that was true. I welcomed that death.

"Yet, I returned, and Brogdon died of fear upon seeing me alive once again. Brogdon's son, Codrin, named me *Pisica Lacrimilor de Sange,* Cat of Blood-tears. Codrin loved me, and it was with him that I shifted from cat to man for the first time."

Archie paused and pushed his red hair from his eyes.

James moved to take his arm. "You must take a break, Archie. This is too mu—"

Archie straightened his back and held up the scepter. "No. I will continue for my son's sake." Archie bent his head and smiled upon the kitten. "He needs the protection this naming ritual will bring to him."

"Okay." James backed away. They all needed the protection of this kitten.

"So mote it be." He jerked his head toward James. "You must repeat those words. Say them now."

James bent his head. "So mote it be."

Archie held his arms wide and continued. "I lived many hundreds of years, and outlived many masters, but when the family and the magic moved to England, I saw Stone Henge for the first time, something shifted at my very core, and I became *Pisica Povestilor,* the Cat of Stories. My role in the magic of the bricks became legendary within the family, and that is what caused my third and fourth deaths. I was murdered by evil men who wanted to steal the magic for their own gain, but I returned each time. That is when I became *Pisica Secretelor*, Cat of Secrets, and my identity was no longer revealed except to the Guardian of the bricks."

James cleared his throat. That was him. He still needed Aunt Eli, but—

Archie cleared his throat and continued. "I lived many hundreds of years, but once trains and automobiles appeared on the roads, I suffered many deaths. In 1895 by a train, when I became *Pisica Magiei Familie,* Cat of the Family Magic. Then death by car in 1901, and again in 1947. I was down to two lives.

"Mistress Eli named me Archibald, Sir Duke of Pisica, and I became the Duke of cats. I was made of the magic in the blood and tears of the bricks. I am one with them, and I am cursed, or blessed with this magical life, because of the love of my original master. Archibald means genuine but also Bold, Brave. That name is the last name I will have." Archie bowed before the bricks that glowed brighter than James had ever seen before.

"All these lessons I have learned through blood and fire, and now, after more than two millennia, I find myself down to one life. The need to name my heir is imminent."

He stood and raised his arms. "With all my names proclaimed, and my role as Protector of the Bricks established, I now grant my heir his first name." Archie raised the kitten with one hand and raised it above his head. "He shall be called Leonardo Alexandru of the Lion Heart, Protector of the artifacts. He will ward off danger and defend his family and the magic as both cat and man. So mote it be."

James repeated, "So mote it be."

Archie sank to the ground, and James knelt by his side. He took Leo from his hand and placed him back on the stool.

"Well done, Archie." James held Archie, who shook

with fatigue. "It's a strong name befitting the role he will have. Are you relieved that you completed the ritual?"

Archie nodded. "And not a moment too soon. I sense Mr. Stickel's mischief, and I must jump within the hour."

Leo raised his head from the footstool and blinked.

****

James glanced out the living room window as the storm whistled through the covered porch and bent trees in the distance. A mew in the hall drew his attention, and he strode across the room. Leo sat in the middle of the dark marble star inlaid in the gray marble of the entry.

He bent down to the kitten, who just stared at him without blinking. Like father, like son. James chuckled and lifted the tiny ginger kit, carrying him into the living room where he sank into the leather wing-backed chair. He winced as Leo kneaded his leg and purred. "You are an important member of this family now. Do you know that?"

He ran a hand down his back. He had dried from the sponge bath after the ceremony to remove the oils. James stared across the living room at the books in a built-in case beside the fireplace. Aunt Eli's house was a stately old home. He should be happy to live here, but he craved his modern Danish couch and faux fur throw rugs.

Leo curled into a ball and fell asleep at once. A sneeze shook the kitten, and James jumped. Leo opened his eyes and scowled.

James chuckled. "So sorry, your highness." He ran his hand over the tiny head. "What is going through your mind, you poor thing?"

Leo hiccupped. James smiled. "Are you going to be like a second child?" He sank back into the chair and closed his eyes.

****

James jerked awake. He'd fallen asleep. He rubbed his eyes. Light poured into the living room. A string of beautiful weather in October wasn't unusual, but he loved the bright days. He searched for wood to knock on so as not to jinx it. He dropped his hands and scanned the room. Where had Leo gotten off to?

"Kitty, kitty?" Where was he?

A crash came from the kitchen. James sprinted across the tree of life carpet, so soft under his feet, and skidded on the slick wood floor. He ran down the hallway, another wool carpet running the length of the hall. Where did Aunt Eli find a rug this long? He skidded into the tiled kitchen.

A toddler sat in the middle of the floor with a cookie jar shattered and cookies scattered all over the black and white tile floor. Chocolate and sugar wafted in the air, and James gasped. Had Leo transformed? Already?

"Where did you come from?" He knelt in front of the baby. He had wet himself and was sitting in a puddle of urine and soggy crumbs.

"Oh my. Come here you little scamp." It must be Leo, but wasn't he too young to transform? Was this normal? James held him up by his armpits.

Leo's face scrunched up, and James braced himself. Here it comes. Leo squirmed from his grasp, and James swung his arms at the air, trying to catch him. What was happening? Where did he go? He stared at the orange kitten on the floor. Leo mewed, then strolled to the door, and sat, then began licking his hind leg. Leo looked up at him once and then returned to his bath.

"Well, thanks for nothing, you." James chuckled. "I suppose you expect me to clean up this mess?"

Leo stood and strolled from the room.

James sank into one of the wooden chairs surrounding the round oak table that sat in a corner of the large kitchen. "Were transformations from cat to human supposed to be that easy?" He rubbed the sleep from his eyes. Or had he just dreamt that?

He glanced at the mess on the floor and grinned. Pulling a whisk broom from the closet, he swept the broken cookie jar and crumbs into the dustpan. Ugh. Cat urine.

He emptied the mess into the trash can. Carol was going to be thrilled.

Chapter Twenty-Seven

Rain pelted the window. Archie yawned. Nice day to curl up on the footstool and nap the day away. Instead, he'd finish the spell that would make Leo his full heir. He glanced at the blanket covering his favorite sleeping spot. He now shared it with his son. He grinned.

He'd always imagined what it would be like to have a son, and heir, but nothing could have prepared him for this outpouring of love. Pushing the blanket from his shoulders, he stood. James stepped to his side. Where had he come from?

"Steady now." James handed him a carved wooden cane with a brass lion's head capping the handle.

He ran his fingers over the smooth wood. How many times had he used this cane? Four times in all. It was the second cane, the first burned in the fire of—

He shuddered. That fire had ended life number three.

A mew came from the footstool. He chuckled. He had fathered many litters but none for an heir. Leo would be his one and only heir, the next Protector of the family and their legacy. He glanced at James.

"We must wake him. He needs to play and exhaust himself, so he sleeps through the ritual of *Tranformatio ad Conscientiam*."

James stooped and ruffled the kitten's fur. Leo crawled up his sweater and onto his shoulder, where he sat watching. James reached his fingers up and the kitten brushed against his cheek. James grinned and set the stool on the table, the blanket dropping off the stool in a wrinkled, cozy bundle.

Archie lifted his arms up to retrieve Leo. "My son." He rubbed noses with the kitten. "This will not hurt, but it will change you in ways you will not comprehend, not in this life but perhaps in the next." Leo mewed and purred. Archie's chest filled until he thought he'd burst. He choked on the words as he whispered, "I love you too, my son."

James turned away, and Archie set the kitten on the floor. He pulled out a stick toy with a ribbon tied to it, as well as three feathers attached to the end. Why did this seem so offensive, so wrong? Was it that Leo was becoming part-human that made this patronizing? No matter. Leo hadn't undergone the ritual yet. Archie jerked the stick, and the feathers danced on the floor.

"Would you like some time alone?" James raised his eyebrows.

Archie dipped his chin in concession. James had a twinkle in his eye. Was it from tears? Respect? No matter. Archie bowed his head and cleared his throat, waving him away with a graceful flourish. He'd have to get a handle on this embarrassment, stigma, self-consciousness, or whatever it was. He was born an animal, just as Leo was, but he'd been forever changed so long ago. He needed Leo to change as well. The more time Leo had to learn and adjust before—

James disappeared up the curve of the spiral stairs.

Archie let the air escape from his lungs.

Alone.

He wouldn't be alone for long, though.

An heir.

Why had he waited so long? He'd craved this for centuries.

"Okay, Leo. Let's get all your wiggles out, shall we?" He twirled the string, and the kitten flew across the room, leaping and scrambling after the feathers.

****

Archie glanced at the table. Leo lay curled in a ball. He called up the stairs. "James? It's time." He waited, then called again. "Ja—"

"Right here." James trotted down the spiral steps, appearing at the bottom. His line of sight on the table.

Archie put a hand on the small copper bowl. "Shall we begin?"

James pointed at the knife on the table and gave Archie a side glance.

"Yes. I'll need human blood to mix with my blood. It should be Sam, but you are here, and she is not." Archie cleared his throat and lifted the blade by the stag horn handle. The edge glinted in the overhead lights. Rain pounded outside the window. "We must complete the ritual with no deviation from the original spell cast by Brogdon, Guillem's oldest son." Archie stopped and blinked twice. "They were so much alike, yet ultimately so different." He sliced the end of his finger. He pressed his finger and let several drops of blood fall into the bowl. He pressed a cotton ball to his finger while James wound tape around it. "Now you."

James held his finger over the bowl. "What is that powder?"

Archie tilted his head and frowned at him. "It's dust from the Roman bricks. All the connections must be made through the original vehicle." James nodded.

Archie pierced the end of James' finger and squeezed several drops of blood into the bowl. He applied the cotton and wrapped it with tape.

"Now for the elixir of *Tranformatio ad Conscientiam,* Transformation to Consciousness." He opened a small vial, and the scent of lavender filled the room.

"That's Latin, right?"

"It is."

James leaned over the table. "Lavender?"

"It's a crucial element to the elixir."

"Is that why the key and book—"

"It is all connected." Archie dropped seven drops of the clear liquid into the blood and mixed it with a wooden spoon, the familiar scent of lavender perfuming the air, and a sense of family, home, and security washed over him like a chamomile balm. *Sit vera voluntas mea.* May my intentions be true. He wished it with every fibre of his being.

He turned to James. "Please present Leo to me. Be careful."

James lifted the tiny kitten and cradled him in the palms of his hands. He extended his arms as the kitten slept on. Archie closed his eyes. Could he go through with this? Was it fair? One droplet escaped his eye as he held back his tears. It tickled as it ran down his cheek. A wave of dizziness ran through him, and he shook his head.

He pointed to the page in the *Tome of Truth.* "Remember, I recite the original and you recite the translation. This firmly connects the past to present."

"Is your part in Latin?"

Archie shook his head. "Why do you not know these

things? You should know—"

James' face lost all color.

"Of course. She ran out of time." He bowed his head. "My sincere apologies."

James gave a clipped nod.

Archie pressed his lips together. Madam Elise hated to relinquish power, not after she had lost Bertha in her unexpected jump through time, but there was no excuse for not preparing the next Guardian. He hissed out a breath and focused on the potion. No regrets, only apologies. So mote it be.

He cleared his throat. "Not Latin. After the escape to the British Isles, Gaelic replaced Latin in most of the spells, so my part, as you call it, is in Scottish Gaelic." It would mean nothing to James, but it meant everything to the spell. If James got his lines right, Leo's transformation would be complete, and the heir would be established. If it was the last thing he did, he'd see his heir by his side, and he would train him, and he would be prepared, no mistakes.

Archie balanced the bowl in the palm of one hand. "It grieves me to do this, son, but one day I hope you will understand and forgive me." He dipped his forefinger in the blood mixture and let a drop fall onto Leo's head. "*Bidh mi a' fosgladh nan ceithir stiùiridhean, tuath, deas, sear, iar.*"

James repeated, "I open the four directions, north, south, east, west."

Archie nodded. James could do this. "*Bidh mi a 'gairm air na ceithir eileamaidean: talamh, gaoth, teine, uisge.*"

"I call on the four elements: earth, fire, air, water." James glanced from Leo, so tiny in the palms of his hands, to Archie. Leo opened his eyes and yawned.

Archie closed his eyes and dipped his finger in the elixir again, running his finger down Leo's back. *"Tha mi a' guidhe air cumhachd na cruinne a bhith a' coimhead thairis orm agus mi a' dol a-steach don àite seo le adhbhar, mo chridhe glan, mo mhiann dìreach math a dhèanamh."*

"I implore the power of the universe to watch over me as I enter this space with purpose, my heart pure, my desire to do only good." James balanced Leo in one palm and put his finger on the faded and discolored paper. He was trying. That's all Archie could ask.

Archie dipped his finger in the blood and ran it the length of Leo's tiny tail. He held James' gaze like a torch to his soul. *"Feumar dìleab an teaghlaich a dhìon, agus tha mi ag ainmeachadh m' oighre dhut, airson mo chuideachadh anns a' cheist seo."*

James cleared his throat and repeated, "The family legacy must be protected, and I proclaim you my heir, to help me in this quest." Leo woke and licked James' hand as well as the elixir from his tail.

"Ann an ainm Guillem an Glic agus a h-uile duine a lean e, tha mi ag ainmeachadh dhut Leonardo Alexandru, Dìonadair nam breigichean, Cruthachadh cat an Leòmhann Chridhe."

"In the name of Guillem the Wise and all the Greats that followed him, I proclaim you Leonardo Alexandru, Protector of the bricks, Cat of the Lion Heart." Archie bent at the waist, a sob escaping. What had he done?

Guillem. He'd never meet his like again. Did his first master ever mean for any of this to happen? No. He hadn't known the vacuum of love and devotion he'd leave behind, but maybe one day they would find a way to end the power of the bricks. Until then—

"You need a break." James bent his head as if in reverence as he held the kitten out. He stood still as a statue.

Archie shook his head. James' arms must ache by now. How could he do this to another creature? "I must finish, as much as it pains me." He wiped a tear from his cheek. "We have only this one chance to enact the spell."

James closed his eyes, and Archie rolled his shoulders, then dipped his finger in the elixir once again. Was it his imagination or had the blood grown thicker? He ran a bloody finger down each leg, and Leo squirmed in James' hands. *"Chun na talmhainn bidh mi a 'leigeil a-mach an lùth seo, agus bidh mi a' dùnadh cearcall a 'chumhachd."*

"Unto the earth I release this energy, and I close the circle of power."

Archie placed his palms together, and James lifted the kitten higher. Leo arched his back. *"Mar sin bidh e,"* Archie whispered.

"So mote it be," James replied

Lightning lit the sky, and thunder rattled the windows of the cellar.

James offered Leo to Archie, and Archie pulled his son close to his heart. Leo stretched his legs out then curled into an even tighter ball. Archie glanced toward James.

"It is done."

Archie pressed his nose into the fuzzy fur ball that was his son. He had survived another death, but he'd be scared for the rest of his life. Hopefully, it was a long life because Leo would need all the training he could get before—

He couldn't even finish that thought.

Archie slipped his hand into the sleeve of a raincoat. "The girls are right on track, but once they catch up with Stickel, we'd better be there for backup." He turned away from James, his scar turning purple. "It's going to get dicey."

James buttoned up his own raincoat. "See you on the other side."

Chapter Twenty-Eight

Sam and Nicole walked arm and arm toward Darlene's townhome. Nicole dodged people as they ran past. Everyone was running in the same direction, toward the smoke. A young man dressed as Wilbert was in a smart blue uniform, directing people who had lined up with buckets as if by magic.

"Wilbert?" Nicole ran to the young man and grabbed his shoulder. He turned, but it wasn't Wilbert. "Where is Wilbert?"

The bobby stared at her. "He's off work, miss, but he might be helping form water brigades and such. Now, if you'll excuse me." He turned to the line. "Oy, you there, mind the water."

Sam took Nicole's arm. "We aren't looking for Wilbert, remember? We need—"

"Right. We need Darlene. I just thought—" Nicole scanned the market. She lifted her arm and pointed down Russel Street. "There." Darlene's red curls bobbed in the distance.

Sam nodded, and the two girls pushed around people and through the crowds. Mr. Stickel's derby bobbed in the crowd, and he had Darlene's arm, her hair shimmering.

Stickel made it to the end of Russel Street and paused to tighten his grip on a flailing Darlene. She smacked his jaw, but he laughed in her face.

Sam pressed her hand to her chest and coughed out smoke. "They're heading to Lincoln Park. Why?"

"He's crazy." Nicole hustled beside Sam, her breathing ragged.

They wove through the crowd as a red truck clanging its bell pushed through the same crowd. Firemen hung from the sides and perched on top. It pulled up to the theater's marquee on Drury Lane, parting the cheering crowd.

Nicole pulled Sam's hand. "He's getting away, and who knows what he'll do to Darlene if he doesn't get the money."

Where was Nicole getting her energy? Sam pumped her legs to catch up. The crowd thinned as they jogged down Drury Lane. Mr. Stickel pulled Darlene along behind him.

"Why doesn't anyone stop him? She's screaming for help." Sam crouched beside Nicole, who'd stopped to let Darlene and Mr. Stickel get around the corner. They could follow that madman, but they couldn't confront him without help. Was Dad coming? Was Archie well enough to jump?

"Why don't we tackle him?" Nicole turned to Sam. "We have to stop him somehow.'

"But, but—"

"But nothing. It's why we're here, right?"

"Nicole—"

"Stop it, Sam. We need a plan. He's getting close to Darlene's townhouse. For once in your life, do the right thing."

"Wha—" Sam's mind whirled. The right thing? Wasn't that what she was doing? She grabbed a branch of the shrub to steady herself. "When haven't I done the right thing?"

"On the Underground Tour, remember? You touched those glowing bricks and started all this time-travel stuff. Now it's not just your world. It's mine too, for some reason, and part of me loves you for it, but the other part hates you." She scrunched up her brow and took off after Darlene and Mr. Stickel.

Sam clenched her fists and counted to three. "Nicole, listen—"

Nicole glanced down the street and gasped. "They've stopped. You better have a good plan by the time we get there, or you better look out."

Sam froze. She couldn't think straight, let alone plan anything, but Nicole meant business. She was screwed.

****

James gasped as Archie wobbled into him. "These jumps get bumpier each time."

"I must concur." Archie held onto James and wobbled. James put a hand on his arm to steady him.

"Aren't we a fine pair." He had to find Sam, but could Archie even walk a block? "Do you know where the girls are? Are we providing backup?"

Archie gave a curt nod. "Eventually. This way." He was bent at the waist as if he was in pain.

James clamped his mouth shut. There was nothing he could do but dash after the still recovering Archie.

Archie halted and put a hand to his temple. "This is the alley that runs to Floral Street, if I'm not mistaken. We turn left at that corner and cross Bow Street. Stickel has Darlene and if my calculations are correct, he is dragging her to her father's townhouse across from Lincoln Park. We must hurry." Archie adjusted his hood and made his way to Floral.

A light mist fell, and James left his hood down. Archie had to be freezing, but he kept moving. Would he be able to complete their mission? James jogged to keep up. Archie stopped in his tracks, and James collided with him.

"What—"

"I sense a change to one of the artifacts." Archie spun on his heel. "Change of plans. Hurry." He let his hood fall down his back and raced away.

Chapter Twenty-Nine

Lincoln's Inn Fields stretched out before them with shrubs and open ground. Sam clutched Nicole's arm as they hunkered behind a tree, waiting for Stickel to make his appearance. Gravel trails crisscrossed the grassy lawns, but no one walked them. Sam loved a quiet park, but she had a sneaking suspicion she wasn't going to experience one today. Nicole hovered beside her, but her body tensed. Now what? Sam followed Nicole's line of sight to the other side of the street.

A row of brownstones faced the park, kind of posh, like Grandma Meyer's in Portland. Wasn't that supposed to mean this was a good neighborhood, like nothing bad could ever happen here?

Mr. Stickel struggled with Darlene as he dragged her to the steps of a majestic brownstone. Sam's skin crawled as Darlene pushed and clawed at the older man. She needed to do something, but what?

"Unhand me." Darlene slapped at Stickel, her cheeks growing rosy.

Sam scanned the park and street. Where were Freddie and Wilbert? They could overpower Mr. Stickel and save Darlene. She couldn't. Nicole pushed to a stand, and before Sam could stop her, she marched out of the park and across Great Queen Street to Mr. Stickel and Darlene.

What was her plan? Did she even have a plan? Oh

Lordy.

Stickel, startled by Nicole's approach, let go of Darlene.

"You." A gleam sparked in his eye. Darlene wriggled out of Stickel's grasp, and Nicole grabbed the arm he raised to strike Darlene.

"No, Nicole." Sam broke a small, supple branch from the oak tree near her, then raced to reach Nicole. Was she too late? *Oh, mama. This was bad.*

****

Archie skidded to a stop as they reached Bow Street. He shook his head as if to clear cobwebs and slapped a hand to his forehead. "No, no, no. We're heading in the wrong direction."

James held his breath. "You said—" He frowned and broke off his sentence.

It was happening just as he'd feared. Archie wasn't ready. He was faltering. These were his own fears causing the confusion, or Aunt Eli's, or—

Maybe this was just how things had to go—utter chaos.

Archie squinted and rubbed his temples. James wanted to put an arm around Archie. It hurt him to see Archie realize he was making mistakes.

"I sense Freddie and Wilbert in that burning building. We have to double back to Traverstock." He turned and rushed back down the sidewalk.

"How do—"

"I taste smoke." Archie sniffed the air.

James grasped Archie's arm. "Sam—"

"You must trust me on this. Sam and Nicole are with Darlene and Stickel. They will be fine, but if Wilbert dies and Stickel isn't stopped, Nicole is in—"

"Big trouble. I get it." James shook his head. Covent Garden was shrouded in smoke that billowed in wispy clouds through the air around them. He didn't have the sight of a protector like Archie did, but Nicole's energy was compromised, as was Archie's. This was a worst-case scenario.

He shuddered. He didn't want this dangerous life of magic for Sam, but it was too late to worry about that. She was in it, and he had to help Archie fix this debacle, or—

His mind raced as he pushed all the horrible outcomes from his mind. He gritted his teeth and followed Archie to the burning building.

****

Sam ran behind Mr. Stickel and whipped his back with her branch.

"Ow." Stickel spun his round face to her, scowling. "You too?"

Sam opened her mouth to respond, but before she could, Stickel, his eyes rolling in their sockets, wrapped his arm around her neck. Was he willing to hurt Darlene? He was desperate enough and insane. She dropped the branch and froze.

"No." Nicole reached for the man.

"Leave her be, or so help me, I'll call the Bow Street Station." A woman dressed in a pale blue dress with a crisp white hat and apron stood with her arms akimbo.

Stickel growled at the woman. "You." He released Darlene, who stumbled into the arms of the woman.

"Nurse?" Darlene beamed at the woman. "Thank the heavens."

Stickel winked at the woman, and Sam did a double-take. Was that a wink? It looked like a wink.

Nurse growled and swung at Sam.

"Don't hurt Sam." Darlene put a hand on Nurse's arm. "She's trying to save me from Uncle Charles."

"These two ruffians?" Nurse glared at Sam then Nicole. "How ever did you make their acquaintance?"

Nicole put both of her hands in the air in surrender. "Call Bow Street Station and ask for Wilbert—" Nicole turned to Sam. "What's his last name? Smythe?"

"Maybe?"

Nurse waved her hand in dismissal. "Just look at you two boys in long pants like young men. Runts both of you."

"Wait. You think we're boys?"

Darlene shook her head. "You aren't boys?"

"No." Nicole stomped her foot. "Do we have to go through this in every time period we jump to?"

Sam cocked an eyebrow at Nicole. "We must dress as boys in order to help Darlene." She explained to Nurse. "We are distant relatives, and we are here to help Darlene get to America and stop Mr. Stickel once and for all."

"Mr. Stickel isn't the problem." Nurse turned to pull Darlene up the stairs into the house.

Sam stepped forward. What did Nurse mean by that?

Darlene put a hand on her arm. "Is Papa home yet?"

"No, miss. He's at the bank finishing his business."

Mr. Stickel lifted his head and sat rubbing his temples. "Is he getting my money?" He chuckled in a cackle that would have frightened a hyena.

Sam glanced down the street. No sign of Dad or Archie yet, so it was up to her and Nicole to finish this. She gritted her teeth and kicked out with her right foot, aiming for his crotch.

"Harrumph." Mr. Stickel doubled over and fell to his side.

"That certainly wasn't very lady-like." Nurse pressed her lips tight.

Darlene wagged a finger at Stickel. "He deserves no less because he's certainly not a gentleman." She scoffed.

Nurse gripped Darlene's wrist in a vise-like grip.

"What? Wait, what are you doing? Unhand me." Darlene tugged.

"This is for your own good, miss." She grinned at Stickel.

Sam's stomach dropped. What was going on between these two? Was Nurse working with Stickel?

Stickel burst to his feet and reached for Darlene. Had he been playing possum? Sam stepped between him and Darlene.

"Get out of my way. You know what I'm capable of." He leered at Sam. "I'm prepared for the ultimate sacrifice this time."

Sam froze. Was he talking about murder?

Darlene jammed her hands on her hips. "Get out of my house, Uncle. You are a fiend. My father will destroy you."

"Will he? Your death will end his bloodline and destroy your father, don't you think? Then I'll finally have justice." His round belly shook as he laughed.

Nicole scoffed. "Justice? For what?" She squeezed Darlene's hand.

Mr. Stickel took a step closer to Darlene, but Sam shoved him hard, and he tumbled down the cement stairs to the sidewalk. He lay in a heap, unmoving.

"Charles. No." She seemed to shrink as she wrung

her hands.

"Don't move." Nicole stood before Nurse.

Darlene sniffed the air and put a hand to her chest as her face grew pale. "I smell smoke. Uncle threatened to start a fire in the theater, but I didn't—"

"Nicole." Sam put a hand to her aching head. Was this part of the magic's effect when information came to her? "We must find Freddie. Now. Something has happened at the theater."

"Oh no. Daddy?" Darlene clasped her hands to her chest.

Nurse scowled and squeezed Darlene's shoulder. Darlene growled as she pushed her hand away. "Don't touch me. How can I trust you after this?"

Nurse cowered. Nicole pushed her toward the house. Without Stickel to guide her, she wasn't a threat.

Darlene took the key ring from her and pointed into the house. "To my room. Let's see how you like being locked up?" She marched the older woman up the stairs with a nod over her shoulder to Sam and Nicole. "I'll be okay. You two go."

Sam gave Darlene a three-finger salute and raised her eyebrows at Nicole. "To the theater." She dashed out the door with Nicole on her heels.

Chapter Thirty

Smoke billowed from the abandoned theater. James coughed and held a hand to his mouth. The clanging of bells rang in the streets as firetrucks pulled up to the smoking building. Was Sam in there? Archie would know, wouldn't he? Archie had a white kerchief held to his nose.

Archie pointed at the theater. "Stickel did this."

"How do you know?"

Archie cocked an eyebrow at him. "You have to ask? He's tampering with artifacts, so of course I know it's him, and I know that Sam is not in there, for your information."

James nodded. Of course Archie knew. James scanned the street crowded with people trying to get out of the area, others wanting a glimpse of the Arcadia Theater. Constables dressed in blue uniforms pressed the crowds back as firefighters ran in and out of the building.

James wiped his eyes, blurred with tears. The smoke stung, but his heart hammered with his anxiety. How could Archie be sure Sam wasn't in there? He watched the doors, looking for something, but what?

Two firemen emerged from the building carrying a stretcher between them. Two more firemen came to their aid, one on each of four poles. Who was being carried out of the building? A dark wool blanket covered a body but not the head. Whoever it was, he was still alive.

James squinted. The person coughed. It was a man.

Archie took a step forward, his hand to his mouth. "That's Wilbert." Archie waved for James to follow as he sprinted toward the burning building. James followed on his heels. How was Archie moving so quickly?

Archie skidded to a stop on Drury Lane. A fire engine blocked the road in both directions, firemen manning hoses directed water on the flames. A fire brigade of Covent Garden merchants and residents passed buckets in a long line of people desperate to contain the fire. James wiped the soot from his eyes.

"Is Wilbert 'G,' the letter—"

Archie sucked air in through his nostrils and stared into space before turning to James. "Yes. I don't know why I didn't see it before. Wilbert is the letter writer. He's the one we were sent to save, not Graham or Frederick Meyer." Archie stared as Wilbert was loaded into an ambulance. He turned to face James. "We need something I don't have. We must return to the throne room."

"What? But I need—" James glanced at the form on the stretcher, then back to Archie.

"No time—"

"Sam—" James leaned against the building.

"This smoke is deadly." Archie wrung his hands, deep furrows creasing his brow. "Wilbert inhaled too much smoke, and if he gets lung fever, he won't survive the journey. We need to make a potion, but the ingredients are in the vault. If he dies, that would be the end of Nico—"

"Right. Let's go." James pressed his fist to his chest. Archie wouldn't leave if Sam was in danger, right?

****

Acrid smoke filled the air, and Sam's lungs stung as she raced down the street. She couldn't keep up with a frantic Nicole who pushed her way through the crowd that had gathered to help. Nicole skidded to a stop.

Sam collided with her. "What are you doing? I—"

"Look." Dark clouds of filthy smoke billowed out of the theater doors. Nicole grabbed Sam by the sleeve as her step faltered. "Oh no. Are we too late?" She pointed to a man being carried on a stretcher. He lay still as death. "Wilbert."

"How do you know that's Wilbert?" The form on the stretcher coughed, and Sam let her breath whistle through her teeth. "He's not dead." Sam pulled Nicole to face her until she nodded that she understood.

Nicole trembled with a sigh. "Yes. Alive is good, but—"

"Wait." Sam frowned. "What about Graham?"

"Didn't Graham say his goodbyes to Darlene?" Nicole stared into space, her face losing all color. If he's not going to America, who is the letter writer?"

Sam pressed her lips together. "Oh—" Sam threw her hands in the air. "So, is Wilbert the missing link? Did you just figure this out?"

"It's weird. I got a tingle in the pit in my stomach." Nicole shook her head, her eyes pleading with Sam.

Sam's brain whirred. Nicole needed her help, not more questions. "Okay. That makes as much sense as anything else to do with the artifacts. What's your plan?"

Nicole stepped forward as two firemen loaded Wilbert's stretcher into the back of a horse-drawn wagon. The wagon pulled away and lumbered down Drury Lane.

"I have an idea, but you aren't going to like it." She

stared after the van.

Sam shrugged. Archie was right. Magic was not a perfect science. "At this point, what choice do we have?"

****

The vault curtains hung open, ties holding them. James hovered outside the vault as Archie mumbled something, rummaging through the vials in a cabinet. If Aunt Eli had begun his training sooner, would he be able to do this? Was he a little jealous that Archie could? Yes.

He could sense the power that once buzzed through his veins begin to fade. The bricks were really choosing Sam over him. He lost power day by day.

He understood. Sam had been drawn to the bricks and used them, not understanding the danger. By the time he'd figured out she had used them and the danger she had put herself in, he couldn't focus. What father could? It was just another reason the bricks were passing him over. He would be nothing more than Archie's assistant now.

"Hold this." Archie pulled out a brown glass bottle with a dropper top. "Coltsfoot." He handed it to James. "Three drops are all we need."

James unscrewed the top and added three drops to a beaker heating over a Bunsen burner.

Archie clanked through the small vials. "Now, lungwort and mullein's root. Where are they?"

"How old is this stuff?" He shook the small bottle. "Did you make all these tinctures and essential oils?"

"Ah ha." Archie ignored his question and pulled out two more vials, handing them to James, who dropped in the ingredients.

"That's the last of them." James screwed the cap on the last vial.

Archie pushed him aside. He let the mixture come to a simmer, then turned off the burner. He poured the potion into a brown bottle that fit in the palm of his hand. "Are you ready? We must get to the hospital and treat Wilbert before his lungs fill with fluid, and he dies."

"Dies? He inhaled a little smoke." James shook his head. Was Archie losing his grip on reality? "Won't they have these same concoctions?"

Dark circles created bruise-like shadows around Archie's eyes. "A little? Remember, we are going to 1929. They don't even have antibiotics, let alone snake oil potions, as they'd call this one." He motioned to James.

James took a step back. "Right."

"If Wilbert develops an infection?"

James held up his hand. "Got it. No need for the gory details."

Archie slipped the bottle into the inside breast pocket of his coat. "Ready?"

James shrugged into his raincoat. "As I'll ever be."

****

Nicole raced to the corner of Drury and Russel Street. She turned left and ran after the wagon that carried Wilbert, his body jiggling and his arm flopping over the side of his stretcher. Sam pumped her legs to keep up. Had he died? He could be dead. The wagon left them behind, and her lungs ached from the putrid air she'd inhaled. She couldn't catch her breath. Nicole never stopped, though, even as exhausted as she had to be. If Sam lost Nicole in this maze of alleys and side streets, she might lose her friend forever.

No. She couldn't let that happen. She cleared her throat and spit. Eww. Gross. It was black.

Was that from the smoke? Already? Wilbert's lungs were full of that stuff. She hadn't even been inside the building, and the smoke had almost leveled her.

Nicole raced through throngs of people in Covent Garden as the wagon wound its way through the market. She paused at Henrietta Street, coughing for air as she peered around the corner of a row of wooden houses. A large brick building stood on the opposite corner at the end of the block. The wagon turned down a driveway opening in a tall brick fence by the brick building.

"Now what?" Sam put a hand on Nicole's shoulder.

She jumped and spun on Sam. "I don't know. Let me think," she snapped.

Sam raised her hands. "Sorry, but we should follow, right?" She peered behind her. Smoke created a dark cloud in the sky that blocked the sun, giving the streets a pall of doom.

"We have to get to him before we lose him in that building." Nicole took off at a sprint to the opening in the fence. She stopped directly across from the driveway and pointed at a sign on the front of the building.

"St. Peter's Hospital?" She gasped. "Oh no. They're carrying him inside." She turned to Sam. "We have to get in there."

Another cart pulled in behind the one that dropped off Wilbert. Sam held Nicole's arm. She pulled. "Let's wait and see what happens with this person. I might have a plan to get us inside."

Nicole spun to face her but put a hand to her head. "Tell me, quick. I'm getting woozy like before."

"What?" Sam grinned at her friend. "Then you're our ticket inside. Put your arm over my shoulder and hang your head like you're about to faint. We're going in."

****

James raced down the alley behind Archie. Where was he finding the energy to run? He'd just died and resurrected himself, right? Archie stopped panting at the corner of Floral.

"They're transporting Wilbert to St. Peter's Hospital."

"How do you know?"

"He is linked to the letter, as am I. I protect the artifacts, remember?" Archie raced headlong through the jumble of shops and alleys that were Covent Garden.

James ran, coughing as he tried to keep up. Smoke hung in the air, a suffocating cloud of toxic metal, wood, and textiles. He put his hand over his mouth and sprinted. Archie turned right onto Harriette Street and a red brick building loomed at the end of the block. Archie pushed through the front door and marched up to a front desk where a broad-shouldered woman in a nun's habit sat scribbling in a ledger. "I'm Dr. Pisica. Where are they taking the fire victims?"

"Oh, Doctor." The nun held her hands in supplication to him. "You truly are a blessing in disguise. You've arrived in our hour of need, you have. Second floor and hurry. It's the staircase at the end of this hall. Take a left at the top of the stairs. You'll see—"

James stared at the woman with the Irish brogue as Archie turned from her and rushed down the hall. That wasn't at all dramatic. James gave her a quick nod as he raced after Archie. Archie had gotten them inside. Maybe James could play the victim and have a coughing fit if they were found out?

Archie glanced over his shoulder at the top of the

stairs, nodded at James, and raced to the left. James followed, clasping a hand to his chest. Was he having a heart attack before his forty-second birthday? He kept Archie in sight as the Protector of the Artifacts hurried through a cavernous room, both walls lined with beds. James scanned each one for Wilbert. Endless beds filled with people coughing, soot-stained clothes polluting the air with smoke and body odor. This was a nightmare straight out of a Dickens novel.

Would they find Wilbert in time? James sidled his way around nurses in white and a doctor with a stethoscope around his neck. No one noticed him or Archie or even tried to stop them.

Chapter Thirty-One

Mr. Stickel opened his eyes and pushed to a wobbly stand. "Did that brat have to push me so hard?" He lifted his derby from the sidewalk and adjusted it on his round head.

"My love," Nurse crooned. "Let me kiss it."

He scowled. Did he really need her? "Where's Dolly?" He adjusted his vest.

Nurse took a step back, her brow furrowed. "I told you never to call her that."

Hmmm. Feisty. Maybe he did still need her. He bowed to her. If he lost her now, he'd never get his revenge. "My lovey, little Dove." Mr. Stickel reached for her hand and kissed the back of it. "It was the fall down the stairs making me peckish. I'm not thinking straight. Where is our Darlene?" He simpered over her limp hand.

Nurse blushed and batted her eyelashes. "I did as you advised. I overpowered her as she was trying to lock me in her room and locked her in there. I left a nice cup of valerian tea for her when she wakes up. She'll sleep for hours."

"Well done, my turtle dove." Mr. Stickel smiled against his will. This would be over soon.

"I was going to check on her, but you can if you wish."

"I wish." Mr. Stickel pulled Nurse to him in an embrace. She giggled in that awful way of hers, and he almost pushed her away, but she giggled and pushed him first.

"Oh, get away, you devil." She giggled as she squirmed from his arms and bustled into the house.

He followed her form as she disappeared. She was a handful, that one, but he was going to be too busy destroying his nephew. He plopped into an overstuffed chair near the parlor fireplace. All he had to do was wait for Freddie to arrive, and he would show his little cousin what defying him would mean for his daughter and every future heir he would never have. Then he'd have the funds to buy that theater, and he could play Achilles, Hamlet, and Henry IV.

He settled into the chair, grinning, and crossing his legs. What was taking Nurse so long?

****

Darlene wobbled to her bedroom window and opened the sash. She leaned out and glanced down the street. How had she ended up in her room? Had she fainted and knocked herself unconscious? Where was Nurse?

Darlene turned and stumbled away from the window and to her nightstand, and a cup of tea. She caught her reflection in the dresser mirror. Her puffy eyes and disheveled hair startled her. She lifted the teacup and inhaled. A sharp tang of stinky cheese hit her nose. Valerian root? Had she been drugged? The cup was full. Had Nurse done this? She put a hand to her head.

"Ow." Tears sprang to her eyes, and she clamped them shut. Where was Daddy?

Light filled the room, even as the sky filled with gray clouds. She tiptoed around her four-poster bed and across the giant wool rug that covered the floor. The fireplace was cold, yet a whiff of acrid smoke hit her nostrils.

Fire. It was coming from Covent Garden. If Father was hurt, she was going to maim that monster. She tried the handle to her bedroom door. Locked, of course.

Uncle Charles's voice croaked a ridiculous song. *Daisy, Daisy, give me your answer do*? A shudder ran through her.

How long had Nurse been working with Uncle Charles? Eww. The man resembled a toad.

She reached for a heavy oak chair next to her door and wedged it under the doorknob. She may be locked in, but Nurse would never get to her. She raced to the window and scanned the street, and gasped.

"Father." He marched toward the house. She slumped against the window frame, her heart pounding. He'd survived. "No." He was walking into danger for her. How did she warn him?

She leaned out her window and waved. How many happy times had she done just this, but now she was doing it to save his life and possibly hers. How did Uncle come to this state of madness, and how could Nurse not see the insanity of his actions? She gritted her teeth. "Uncle Charles."

A soft knock came on her door. "Miss?"

"Nurse." She rushed to the door and put her hands against it. If she could reach through the wood, she would wring Nurse's neck, she would.

"Your door is stuck, miss. Let me in." Her simpering voice hit Darlene's ears like a sledgehammer.

She scoffed at the door. Did Nurse think she was still drugged? Let her rot. She ran back to the window and leaned farther out the window and called. "Father." He did not respond, and she dared not raise her voice any louder.

He glanced to the window, his eyes shining as they met hers. She opened her mouth to speak, but he broke into a dead run. She didn't have a chance to warn him. She crossed her fingers. Everything would be fine, right?

Nurse knocked on the door again, more insistent this time. "Time to wake up, miss."

Darlene had to do something to distract Uncle Charles before Father broke down the front door. She balled her hands into fists and raced to the chair. She slipped it from under the knob, turned the latch, and yanked it open. Nurse took a step back.

"Oh my."

The element of surprise had worked. She scowled at Nurse. "What's wrong? Were you expecting me to be afraid?"

"No, miss, I-I—"

"Don't miss me." Darlene scooped a vase off a table by the door to her room, and in one fell swoop, cracked Nurse on the side of her head. Nurse gave out a squeak as she dropped like a stone. Darlene pulled the house keys from her pocket, slipping them in her own.

Uncle called, "Betty? Did you break something? Is everything going to plan up there?" His footsteps sounded on the marble entry. Was he climbing the stairs? She held her breath.

Should she try to imitate Nurse's voice? No. He would not be fooled. She put her hands to her cheeks. Stickel huffed and puffed up the steps and stopped halfway to gape at Darlene.

"How did you—" He raced to the top step and gasped. "No." He took a step back. "You didn't have to kill her." His face dissolved into a grimace.

Darlene shook her head. What a moron. "Enough. I'm tired of your deceits. She's unconscious, Uncle."

He bent to Nurse's side, patting her hand, and Darlene scooted past his bent form. She closed the door and locked it behind her, then ran across the landing to the stairs.

Betty? How had she never learned Nurse's name? No matter, she was a traitor. Darlene reached the stairs and raced to the bottom. Father's key fumbled in the lock. He pounded his fist on the front door, and she was at the door, turning the deadbolt. He burst inside and embraced her until she couldn't breathe.

"Oh, my darling. I feared the worst. Are you okay?"

"I'm fine, Father, but how about you?" She ran her hands over his shoulders and chest. "You escaped the fire, but your clothes." She pulled out a hanky and held it to her nose. "You'll be happy to learn Stickel is upstairs with Nurse."

"That's good news, but—"

She glanced over her shoulder. "Where is Wilbert?"

Freddie's shoulders slumped. "I had to get to you. I thought he was following me—"

"What?" She turned, still holding the lavender scent to her nose. "You left him?"

Father's voice broke into her reverie. "Stickel is trying to destroy our family. I had to find you—"

"But Wilbert."

Freddie nodded. "First things first. I must call Bow Street Station. Surely, they have cause to arrest Uncle Charles now. He needs to be in a cell at Bow Street Station, then to Bethel Royal."

Darlene nodded, her eyes tearing. "The looney-bin,

perfect. He's upstairs with his accomplice." She pointed to the stairs. "But you'll need help, won't you?"

"Accomplice?" He scowled at her.

"Nurse. Did you know her name was Betty?"

"No, I did not." He ran his hand along her cheek. "But I don't care. Nobody abducts my daughter and gets away with it." He sniffed. "I thought I'd lost you."

She smiled up at him. She closed her eyes. "Uncle Charles has been colluding with Nurse Betty. Can you believe that?"

"I can now." Father walked to the phone on a table in the entry. "I never did like her anyway. She'll have to be questioned, too." He dialed a number, the rotary dial clicking as it spun.

****

James had to lengthen his steps to keep up with Archie. Where was he finding his strength, anyway? Archie hesitated, then came to a complete stop beside a bed where a soot-covered man in a wool navy coat lay, his face blackened. Was it Wilbert under all that soot? He couldn't tell.

"His breathing is shallow, as is his pulse." Archie pulled out the vial. He unscrewed the stopper as a nurse in a nun's habit bustled down the row of beds.

James rubbed his forehead with his right hand and sloughed out of his wet coat. He slung it over his arm, and nodding to Archie, he moved down the row toward the oncoming Nun. If he didn't stop her, Archie wouldn't be able to revive Wilbert, and he was their only chance at stopping Stickel's evil scheme.

James cleared his throat and stuck out his hand to shake hers. "Hello."

She recoiled and stared at his hand. "What in God's

good name do you think you're doing?" She moved toward Archie.

James stood his ground. She was a battle-ax if there ever was one. He gave a small bow. "I'm Dr. James Stevens—"

"I don't care if you're the Pope, young man. What are you doing to this patient?" She burned him with a scathing stare.

"Umm, my associate—"

Archie put a hand on James' sleeve. "Madam, I apologize for the confusion. We were just leaving." He took James' arm and steered him back toward the door.

"But, but—" The nun stuttered and rushed to the patient.

James strode after Archie as they pushed through the crowd of smoke-singed people in the entry and burst out the front doors. Archie trotted down the steps, and James followed.

"Did you administer—"

"Of course I did." He grinned over his shoulder. "Now to Covent Garden to stop Stickel."

Chapter Thirty-Two

The steps to St. Peter's were not steep or many, but Sam could not help Nicole climb them. She was weak, a dead-weight. Was she going to pass out?

"Nicole." Sam held her arm as Nicole sank onto the bottom step. Sam's mouth went dry. She sank beside Nicole and put her arm around her shoulder. Nicole shivered.

"Are you okay?" Stupid question. Of course she wasn't okay.

Nicole nodded. "Just give me a minute. The dizziness is passing."

The hair on Sam's neck stood on end. She scanned the street filled with smoke from the theater fire, the acrid air burning her throat. A man in a dark trench coat hovered in the shadows across the street. He stepped off the curb and headed toward them, the hairs on her arms tingling.

"Isn't that Archie?" She turned to face Nicole, whose expression softened.

"What just happened?" Nicole wiped her brow with the back of one hand.

Archie walked to them, and Sam rose to her feet.

Before he reached them, Nicole blurted out, "We're in the wrong place, aren't we?"

"What?" Sam shook her head. How could Nicole know that?

"You've saved Wilbert, but Darlene is in trouble again."

Sam stared at Nicole. What was up with Darlene, now? Couldn't she stay out of trouble for ten minutes?

Archie tilted Nicole's face up and tried to establish eye contact. "You are correct. How are you feeling?"

Goosebumps developed on Sam's arms. Archie's behavior grew stranger by the minute.

Nicole jerked her head away from him and swayed to her feet. "Whatever caused the dizziness has passed."

Archie blinked. "You must return to Lincoln Park immediately."

"Wait." Sam sank to Nicole's side. She glanced over her shoulder, but Archie had disappeared. Nicole brushed dust from her pants, then headed down Harriet Street without a backward glance.

Sam put a hand to her head. Who was the Guardian of the Artifacts right now? The letter was connected to Nicole's family, and Nicole was of the blood.

Nicole was halfway down the block, and Sam called, "Nicole, wait up."

Did this mean Nicole was the Guardian?

****

The sun shone through the beveled glass in the wooden doors to cast diamond rainbows across the floor of the Meyer residence. Freddie leaned against the phone table near the stairway and stared at the colors. Trunks and crates were stacked on the marble floor, ready for the steamship liner's crew to fetch and stow them in their state rooms. If they made it on board, that was.

He closed his eyes. Would his departure save his family from his revenge rampage?

The dark star inlay in the lighter marble of the floor

impressed him as it always did, the perfect choice by his ancestors for their family symbol of hope, a sign of guidance. He gripped the phone tighter as pounding boomed from upstairs. Stickel would break the door down if the bobbies didn't hurry.

"Bow Street Station."

"Yes. I'd like to report a crime." He stared at Darlene, his beautiful daughter. All he wanted to do was protect her.

"Can you stay on the line for a moment, sir?"

"Yes, I'll wait." Soon, this would all be a bad memory they could put from their minds.

Darlene waited by the luggage, her trust in him shining on his face. She was fearless, this child of his. Freddie cleared his throat. "Does Mother know you left the hotel room?"

"Of course not." She played with the ribbon at her waist as she scanned the crates and luggage, then out the front door that hung open, its frame splintered. "She never would have let me go. But then again, I didn't think—"

Her voice wobbled, and he winced. How could he leave without knowing Charles was behind bars once and for all? His chest tightened.

"Sir? Are you there?"

"Yes." Freddie winked at Darlene.

"Right, sir. Might I have your name, your location, and the nature of your call, please?"

"Of course. This is Mr. Frederick Meyers III, and I'd like to report a break-in. My location is 16 Lincoln's Fields. There are two—"

A scuffle stopped Freddie mid-sentence.

"Sir?" the man on the voice called.

Freddie dropped the phone. "No."

Mr. Stickel grabbed Darlene's right arm and pushed past Freddie. Darlene stumbled over the luggage and through the door.

"You can't stop me, Freddie. Just give in, or she dies." Stickel's laugh followed him out the entry, down the steps.

"My sweet child." He rushed out the door.

A light pounding began, and Freddie glanced at the landing above them. Charles had locked Nurse in.

Freddie leapt down the stairs and spotted Uncle Charles waddling down the sidewalk, Darlene in tow.

Freddie raced after them, scanning the road and the buildings as he ran.

Gone. What would Constance say? Charles was out for revenge, blaming Freddie for his financial ruin. He would never leave his family alone. Had booking passage to America been a mistake? No. He had to leave London, but first, he had to end Charles' dominion over him once and for all.

Charles appeared farther down Long Acre and turned into another brownstone. Freddie's pulse stopped. "Darlene," he called, then took off at a sprint.

****

Sam jogged down Long Acre behind Nicole, brownstone buildings passing in a blur. What was she doing? Did she sense a change? Was this a magical inspiration? Nicole increased her pace.

Sam's stomach tightened. Nicole couldn't keep up this pace, but they were running out of time. The crash of the stock market would happen soon, and Darlene had to be on that ship bound for America. If they didn't catch Stickel in time, Darlene might never marry, and her bloodline would disappear. Did that mean Nicole would disappear?

Nicole stopped on the sidewalk. "Stickel," she said with a gasp.

Sam followed her finger and tensed. Mr. Stickel disappeared into a run-down house, pushing Darlene before him. He slammed a door with red paint flaking onto the porch. A crack in one of the street-side windows and cobwebs hanging from the ceiling told a story of neglect and disrepair.

Stickel had squandered his mother's fortune, and he'd bankrupt Freddie if he wasn't stopped.

"We have to stop him." Nicole panted and tottered toward the house as Freddie arrived.

"Are they—" Freddie skidded to a stop.

"Yes. Mr. Stickel and Darlene are—" She pointed with a limp hand to the house.

"That's his house. My great aunt would roll over in her grave if she could see how he'd let it fall into decay." Freddie pushed them aside and rushed inside.

Sam scoffed. "He destroys everything he touches." If she had anything to say, Mr. Stickel was going to the insane asylum, and she would help put him there.

Nicole reached for the stair railing to the house and sank to the ground.

Sam sank to her side. "What's wrong? We have him cornered. Get up."

Nicole shook her head. "No strength. You have to stop him. Quick."

"What?" Sam couldn't do this without Nicole, could she? She rubbed her arms that were tingling again.

She lifted Nicole to her feet. "We're not finished." Sam held Nicole's gaze. "I don't know what is happening, but it must be tied to the letter." Was it the letter making Nicole dizzy and weak? Sam reached inside her shirt for the letter. She patted her pockets. Had she dropped it? No. Archie must have—

She slung Nicole's arm over her shoulder. "Everything is going to be fine. We will fix this." She heaved Nicole's weight onto her.

"I'm dizzy." Nicole put a hand to her forehead.

Sam inhaled a shaky breath. "I know, but this is how you stop it. Your family is counting—"

"Why can't Freddie fix this?" Nicole glared at Sam.

"He's here. He's trying—"

A woman's scream came from the house.

"Darlene?" Nicole held Sam's gaze.

She helped Nicole up the stairs. "We're almost finished. I promise."

****

James closed the stationery shop door. He gripped the parcel of paper. The pen and ink made it awkward to run as he carried it all in his hands. When did they invent shopping bags anyway? Archie stood on the corner, leaning against the wall, waiting for him.

"Did you get everything I asked for?" He frowned at James.

"Yes, but do we really have to return to St. Peter's?"

"If we want to save Nicole, yes." Archie furrowed his brow. "Wilbert must write the letter so that we can deliver it."

"Oh. The original—" James waited as Archie swallowed and pushed away from the wall. He was clearly exhausted and wouldn't make up a wild goose chase if it weren't going to stop the damage to the space-time continuum. He stuffed the supplies in his coat pocket. "Let's get back to Wilbert. We can bring the girls home with us, right?"

"The girls will come home when it is time, but for now, they still have their own part to play, but time is running out. Whatever happens, they only have until midnight. That's the twenty-four-hour mark."

James did a double-take. "What? You never mentioned a time limit. Does Sam know that?" James clutched the paper to his chest.

"I've been a little busy dying and coming back to life. Besides, we have all the time we need if we don't waste a minute of it. I have no doubt Sam and Nicole can meet the temporal constraints." He nodded and, with that pronouncement, turned and hustled around the corner onto Harriett Street.

James shrugged. The pull of the artifacts grew weak within him. Was Sam up to this challenge? Did any of them have a choice in this magical process? He jogged to catch up to Archie, a shiver vibrating down his spine.

Chapter Thirty-Three

Sam raised dust as she helped Nicole up the steps, creaking with their weight. Would it hold them? The sheers hanging in the entry window were torn and yellowed with age. She supported Nicole as they took one step at a time. "Now I feel dizzy."

Nicole wobbled. "Me too, but Darlene is in there."

"Wait." Sam pushed past Nicole. The boards groaned, but Sam ignored them.

The front door stood ajar, and she swung it wide, the hinges creaking. Why was it so quiet? She stepped into the entry and stopped at the dark star shaped marble pattern, the same star as one in Darlene's entry, Grandma Meyer's, and her own at Aunt Eli's. A tingle raced from the back of her head to her shoulders.

Voices filtered down into the hallway from a room upstairs. Freddie, Darlene, and Stickel shouted and yelled over one another. She couldn't make out what they were saying, but it was about money, she was certain of it.

Freddie and Darlene needed help. She scanned the foyer for a weapon, a board, a—

She clasped a metal-handled umbrella leaning against the wall. It sported a brass duck head with a prominent beak. "Stay here, Nicole."

She gripped it and took the stairs two at a time, stopping at the top. Darlene's muffled crying and

Freddie's pleading blended with Stickel's angry voice. Sam eased down the hall and peeked through the cracked door. Mr. Stickel stood with his back to her. She had a clear shot of the back of his head.

She inhaled, pushed the door open, and lifted the umbrella. Could she do this? Did she have a choice? She closed her eyes and stabbed with the umbrella handle. A cry from Stickel tightened her stomach. She cracked an eye open and watched Mr. Stickel slumped to the floor, groaning with his hands to his belly.

Her hands shook, but she tugged at a cord that tied back the curtains and handed it to Freddie. "Hurry. We have to go."

He took the cord from her and tied Stickel's hands behind his back. "I have some unfinished business to take care of here." He stood with his arms folded across his chest. "Take Darlene to the White Falcon. I'll follow you once the police have Uncle Charles in custody." He gave Sam a curt nod.

"Father." Darlene planted her feet and refused to leave.

"Go, quickly. I'll meet you at Peebles'." He kissed her forehead.

Sam nodded to Freddie. "We'll keep her safe." Taking Darlene's hand, she raced down the stairs with Darlene behind her.

Nicole stood at the bottom.

Sam took one of Nicole's hands and Darlene took the other. "Quick. Freddie's with Stickel until the police get here. We have to get Darlene to safety." They hobbled down the steps. "Can you run?"

Nicole had that deer-in-the-headlights look. "Do I have a choice?"

207

Sam couldn't respond. They didn't have a choice. Darlene led the way, and Sam followed with Nicole as she turned down the first alley on the right. Smart move if Stickel got past Freddie, he wouldn't know where they'd turned. Hopefully, he didn't get past Freddie. Again.

****

Darlene raced down an alley. Sam inhaled the smoky air and coughed. They were back in Covent Garden, but where was Peebles'? Darlene stopped, and Nicole pressed her back against a wooden building, her breath coming fast. Darlene paced in the cramped alley, her hand pressing against her chest.

Sam bent at the waist, her hands on her knees. "Are we safe here? What's our plan?"

Nicole closed her eyes and sank to the ground. "If Stickel has succeeded in—"

Sam put her finger to her mouth, and Nicole clamped her lips tight.

Darlene sagged against the wall beside her. "I don't understand Uncle Charles. Why is he doing this?"

Sam scratched her head. What did she say to Nicole's great ancestor, or whatever? "Are you getting any tingles from the artifact?"

Nicole put a hand on her chest. "I'm not getting any directions or 'feelings' like I did before." Nicole made air quotes around feelings. "Do you think I lost my connection to the letter? Is it because I'm disappearing?"

Darlene stomped her foot. "What are you talking about? Disappearing? Artifacts? Who are you two?"

A chill ran through Sam's body. She shot Darlene a side glance. "We'll explain it all later, but for now, we need to get off the streets and formulate a plan."

"I agree." Darlene pointed to the shop sign. "We're at Peebles' Pretties Toy Shoppe. We can wait for Father in the cellar."

Sam glanced at Nicole. "In the cellar? What do you think?"

Nicole shrugged. "It's where I landed, and it's close to where Sam landed. It should be perfect, if the bricks cooperate."

Darlene pressed her lips into a thin line, then spoke. "Hugh, the stockboy, let me hide in the cellar once when Uncle Charles first started all this revenge fiasco." Darlene closed her eyes. "He's been a godsend."

Sam tilted her head to see down the alley. "When Freddie arrives, we can make a plan to get you to the docks. This could all be over soon." Sam smiled.

Nicole pushed herself to stand. "I'll stay with Darlene here."

"Rest." Sam gave a quick nod. "I'll watch for Freddie from the alley."

"Right-o." Darlene reached for Nicole's elbow. "I'll get her to the stockroom before she passes out."

****

Sam hunkered in an alley across the street from Peebles'. She leaned against the wall in the shadows as a young man walked out the shop door and strolled in her direction. Here we go. Just be cool.

"Can I help you—" He had a warm smile and relaxed stance.

"Are you Hugh?"

"I am, but who—"

"I am Sam, and Darlene Meyer and my friend Nicole are in your cellar. We're waiting for Mr. Meyer." Sam wrung her hands. Why was she so nervous? She stuffed her hands in her pockets. Could she trust Hugh? Did she have a choice? "Can you help us?"

"Of course. How can I be of service?" He closed the distance between them.

"Just make sure they are safe."

He smiled at her and gave a curt nod with his head. "Certainly. Your friends are safe with me."

Sam blinked. That was too easy. Was Hugh telling her what she wanted to hear? She took in his clean but baggy pants and his unbuttoned vest over a cotton shirt. He was slight for a young man, but he stood as tall as she was. She couldn't wrestle him to the ground if she had to, and a shiver ran down her spine. Had she just walked into a trap?

She held her breath until Hugh disappeared into the toy shop. She paced the alley. Freddie should be here by now. She scanned Covent Gardens, hoping his tall, distinguished form would appear. She gasped. Two men were marching down the street toward her. She froze.

"Dad?" She took a step out of the alley. He and Archie slowed as they approached.

"Sam?"

"Oh, Dad." She rushed to him.

He pulled her into a hug. "I wasn't sure where you were or—" He held her at arm's length before releasing her.

Her stomach tied into a knot. "Something's up. What is it?" She tensed.

"We were heading back to the hospital when we spied you—"

"Wilbert?" She shook her head. "How is he?"

"I had to administer a potion, but he'll recover." He blinked at Dad. "We must go."

"Where to?"

"Wilbert has one more letter to write. Where's Darlene?"

"She's in Peebles' Toy Shoppe with Nicole. Do you want—"

Archie shook his head. "No. We must hurry, James. Wilbert is our only hope."

Dad gave Sam a grim smile and rushed to catch up with Archie, who was already halfway down the block. Sam stood in the street as people shoved around her in both directions. She was alone in a crowd of people who didn't even notice her. Wagons clattered on the cobblestones, the racket grating on her nerves.

Freddie stopped to join her on the street. "Nicole and Darlene?"

She nodded. "They're fine."

"Good." He stared at Peebles' Pretties Toy Shoppe. "Nurse escaped before the police arrived."

Sam gasped. "What? How—"

Freddie frowned. "It doesn't matter how. It happened, and now I need to find Mr. Stickel before he hurts someone. Have you seen him?"

"No." Sam stared at Freddie.

He turned to the shop. "He's hell bent on revenge, and he won't stop until—"

He turned on his heel and rushed away, scanning every alley as he went.

Did he think he could take on Stickel alone? She raced across the street. Freddie was obviously no match for Stickel.

Nope.

Chapter Thirty-Four

The tang of rubbing alcohol filled the air and made Archie's nose twitch. He missed his whiskers while he was in human form, but he'd be able to shift back to cat-form soon enough. Just one more task. This mission weighed on him like a lead coat.

He marched into St. Peter's Hospital. He knew where he was going, and in his annoying fashion, James hovered to catch him in case he stumbled from fatigue. Did James think he was going to fall? He walked the full length of a sterile white hall, windows on two walls letting in light covered in sheers, for what, privacy? To shield the patients from what, the fog?

Archie straightened his spine and pushed his shoulders back as he hurried past a nun, who raised a hand, her mouth opened to speak. Archie ignored her, hoping he exuded confidence. He was portraying a doctor after all, and his presence should go unquestioned, unless—

He walked to Wilbert's bedside.

"Is Wilbert strong enough for this?" James took in the soot on the young man's face and the blue lips. "Is he getting enough oxygen?"

"He is growing stronger by the minute." Archie leaned over Wilbert's still form. He sensed a strong heartbeat and placed a hand on the young man's shoulder. Wilbert raised his hand and clasped his fingers around Archie's. James waited as Wilbert formed words, but a coughing fit soon wracked his body.

James shuffled his feet. "What did he say?"

"He couldn't finish. The coughing." Archie stared at Wilbert. "He doesn't want us to leave, but why?"

James moved closer to the bed. "He needs to write that letter and get to the docks in time to—"

Wilbert pulled Archie to him, and he put his ear close to Wilbert's lips.

"Help me up," Wilbert whispered.

"Certainly. That's why we're here. You know what you must do, don't you?"

Wilbert closed his eyes and nodded, a sigh shuddering through his body.

"Quick." Archie held his hand out to James, who handed him the pen and paper. "You must pen a new missive."

Wilbert tried to sit up but fell back on his pillow in a fit of coughing. Archie winced as Wilbert recovered his strength and croaked, "How did you know?"

"Because, my dear, this letter will solve all our problems." Archie held the paper and pen as rain splattered on the glass.

"I already sent her a missive, as you say, but she didn't reply." Wilbert closed his eyes. "Did the letter reach her?"

"It did not, and that is why we are here. Darlene must get this letter. Stickel is desperate for money, and he knows where she is."

Wilbert nodded to Archie. "Help me. I'll write it now."

Archie smiled at Wilbert. A calm filled his body, like a hot cocoa on a snowy day. Wilbert began to scratch out letters on the paper. He folded the paper and slipped it in the envelope. With a sigh, he handed it to Archie. Was that a glint in his eyes? Archie smiled. Wilbert had grit. Now they had to get the letter to Darlene.

Archie slipped the letter in his inside coat pocket and turned to James. "You must get Wilbert to the pier by yourself while I deliver the letter. I'll head to Peebles' Pretties to assist Sam. Freddie and Darlene must be on that boat."

"So, this letter will solve—" James' shoulders sagged.

Archie hesitated. They all had "jump-fatigue."

He put a hand on James' arm. "Yes. The letter slipped out of a bag, so Darlene never received it, and the scenario that Stickel set in motion caused Wilbert to miss the boat. The letter Nicole received has disappeared to account for the overlap in time. Understand?"

James nodded. "I'm trying."

"He wrote a new letter, and she must receive it. Then you must make sure he arrives in time to make that voyage. I'll see that Darlene gets the new letter." Archie wobbled and leaned against the side of the bed, and James took a step toward him.

"You're too weak." James reached out a hand.

He waved James away. "No. I'll be fine. This is writ on the pages of *The Tome of Truth.*"

James did a double-take. "*The Tome*—"

"Get him to the docks. He'll know what to do."

Archie furrowed his brow. James wouldn't be the Guardian, but he didn't have to be dense as brick, did he? Archie stormed away in a swirl of black jacket and scarf, a little dramatic, but how else did he get James to act.

****

The shadows in the alley hid Sam as she crouched, watching the street. Two people approached at a run, and her throat constricted. Could it be? She'd left him unconscious at his mother's house.

It was him. Stickel and Nurse Betty charged to the door that led to the stockroom. How had they found Darlene so fast? Her head spun. How did she warn Nicole?

Hugh stood in the open door and waved him inside. What the heck? Was he working for Stickel now? Sam opened her mouth to berate him, but that wouldn't help the situation.

Hugh.

She clenched and unclenched her fists. What a worm.

Stickel held the door for Betty like the dandy he wasn't, and they disappeared into the building. Sam buried her face in her hands. Now what? Nicole and Darlene were sitting ducks, and Stickel wouldn't hold back now. If he got past Freddie, he was capable of anything. Sam had to get to the door and catch it before it latched shut and locked.

A dark figure got to the door before her. Archie. His unmistakable red hair peeked out from under his derby. She called to him, but he slipped inside without turning to acknowledge her. She ran to the door, but it clicked shut before she reached it. She pounded and stepped back as the door swung open. Archie scowled at her.

"Shhh." He jerked his head for her to step inside. "We need the element of surprise."

She stepped in and let the door close behind her, softening the click so neither Stickel nor Hugh would hear it.

Archie held a finger to his lips. She nodded and followed him down the stairs on tiptoes.

Stickel's voice reverberated off the walls. "Your dear old dad will give me all the money I need. Now come with me, dear." He spoke with authority, but the thinly veiled insanity rang through to her.

Sam pressed against the wall of the stairwell. Does he think he's won this battle? Because he hasn't.

"You can't do this, Uncle."

"Do what? Claim my birthright? Rise to fame on the stage?" His feet scraped against the dusty floor as he ranted.

He was coming unglued. She had to get to Nicole before he hurt her.

"You know that Sam will be here soon with the police. You realize what that means, don't you?" Nicole's voice wavered, but she was standing her ground.

Sam pushed away from the wall, but Archie held up a hand. He shook his head. Did he expect her to wait on the steps, because if he did—

"Sam is dead." Stickel's maniacal voice shook off the walls, and his eyes rolled in his head. He paced the stockroom in short steps, twisting to pace the other direction.

Dead? What? Would Nicole believe those words? Did Stickel?

"Dearest, you must—" Nurse's voice pleaded. Did she recognize his behavior as madness?

"I must what? Calm down? I've won. This secures the funds for my—"

Archie snuck down the stairs but tripped over a box between him and Stickel. Sam's stomach twisted. Archie never tripped. Was he still weak? Could he complete this mission? She raced down the steps to him.

"Archie." She grabbed his arm, but he shook her off.

"Well, well, well. If it isn't my old pal Archibald, the Duke of, what was it? Ah, yes, the Duke of Pisica, the Duke of Cats." Stickel chuckled, wringing his hands.

Sam scanned the subterranean room. Light filtered through the dirty windows high on the stockroom walls. A dim lantern sat on a table, exposing Hugh, who slunk to the stairs, rushed up them, and dashed out into the alley.

"Good riddance." Darlene shook her fist at the stairs Hugh had just scurried up. "You rat."

Nicole's fierce expression brought a calm to Sam's psyche. She braced herself to help Archie, even if it meant tackling Stickel.

Archie stood his full height and stared Stickel down. "Charles, this is over. The police will be here soon."

Stickel jammed his fists on his hips and laughed. "You have no control over this situation, Archibald. Not this time. I have Freddie's precious daughter."

"You're a monster." Darlene scowled at him. "Father will find a way—"

"To what? Stop me?" Stickel giggled. "He's a little tied up at the moment." He hooked his thumbs in his lapel and rocked on his heels. "When Hugh sent word you were here, well, what a stroke—"

"This was not a stroke of luck." Sam spat the words at him. "Not for you anyway. I'm going to stop you this time, for once and for all."

"Charles, what is she—" Betty held her hand to her chest, her eyes on Charles.

"Oh, shut up, Betty." Stickel pushed her aside as he

strode to Sam.

"But—but Charles." Betty put a hand to her chest. Her eyes turned soft with confusion.

Sam leaned forward, ready to pounce, but Archie moved between them and grabbed Stickel's wrist. He mumbled some words, and Stickel grew pale, then fell to the ground unconscious.

"Charles?" Betty spun toward Archie. "What have you done?"

"I stopped him." He winked at Sam and shrugged.

Sam stood transfixed. He'd said that magic wasn't an exact science, but that was a new one, one she needed to learn.

"Charles," Betty moaned.

"He's in a trance, but he will wake soon." Archie scanned the room and strode to Darlene. He took her hands in his. "Darlene, you must go with Sam and Nicole. They will help you return to your mother. If my calculations are correct, she hasn't missed you yet. Tell her you went out for tea if she asks."

Darlene nodded. "But what about Father? And Wilbert? Should they be here too?"

Archie handed her a letter in a familiar hand. Was it from Wilbert? Darlene took the letter and opened it. She read it and gasped, a blush rising from her neck to her cheeks. She pressed the letter to her heart. "'G' is Wilbert?" She closed her eyes as she slipped the letter in her purse.

A shudder shook the building, and the hair on Sam's arms stood. Was this the shift they'd all been waiting for? She glanced at Nicole. Was it her imagination, or was the color returning to her cheeks? Archie nodded his satisfaction.

"Freddie will be here soon." He waved at Stickel, still unconscious on the floor. "Nicole, Sam, we must hurry. James is bringing Wilbert."

"I had no idea." Darlene shook her head. "All this time I thought it was—"

"Love is a mystery." Archie blinked at her. "But now we must go."

"But what about her?" Sam stared at Betty.

"Let her stay." A smile tugged at Archie's lips.

"I have a few choice words for Mr. Charles Mortimer Stickel, Esq." Betty crossed her arms over her chest.

Chapter Thirty-Five

Sam took one last glance at Stickel and Betty before rushing up the stairs after Archie. Sam wanted to hang Stickel from the tallest rafter, but murder was against the family motto: *Misericordia et Justitia*, Mercy and Justice. Fine.

Archie skidded to a stop in the alley. "Freddie is making his way to the docks."

"Father didn't wait for me?" Darlene stared her mouth open.

"I sent him on before anything else could go wrong."

"How do you know everything is going right?" Nicole asked as she and Darlene hurried to catch up.

He raced down the street. "I'm the Protector of the artifacts, remember?"

Really? That was his response? Sam took a step as a white slip of paper poked out of Archie's pocket. It jiggled as he raced down the sidewalk until it floated to the ground. She ran to it and picked it up. Another artifact? A hint of lavender tickled her nostrils.

"Archie?" She waved the paper, but he ignored her, as a jolt of electricity or something tingled from her fingers to her shoulder and left a warmth in the pit of her stomach. She held the paper by her fingertips, careful not to drop it. The tingling eased a bit. "Archie?"

He was winding through Covent Garden, to a raised

tram platform. The sign read: COVENT GARDEN. His focus was on getting Darlene to her parents' hotel near the docks. She slipped the paper into her pocket and jogged to catch up.

Archie stopped at a ticket counter and paid their fare. He handed them each a ticket, and all four of them stepped onto the platform. A tram squeaked to a stop, and Archie motioned to a seat for Darlene and Nicole. Sam slumped onto the wooden bench across from them as Archie reached in his pocket and his mouth dropped. He jumped to his feet.

"Looking for this?" Sam pulled the slip of paper from her pocket.

He gasped. "How did you—"

"It fell from your pocket as we ran to catch the tram. I called, but you kept running." She waited for an explanation.

He nodded and his gaze burned into her. "You may have saved us all. These words will ward us from—"

"From what this time?" Nicole held Darlene's hand.

He held up the paper. It was in Latin or Gaelic or some other language she wasn't familiar with. "After we return Darlene to her parents, she will be safe, and Nicole's future will be too, but the bricks are never safe as long as Stickel lives. Without this spell, he could use them again."

Nicole slumped in the seat. "Of course, it always comes back to Stickel. When will he stop once and for all?"

Archie grimaced. "Freddie must play his part now." He blinked at Sam. "Once we return home, I must recite these words to nullify the magic in the bricks, so Stickel cannot use them."

Sam tucked loose hairs behind her ear. "So, is that spell from the *Tome of Truth*?"

"It is." He gave her one quick nod.

"You should rest, Archie. You're still recovering." Sam patted his elbow, and he leaned back in his seat.

"Thank you, child." He handed her the paper.

Sam opened the note but shook her head. "What language is this?"

"It's Scottish Gaelic, the language of your ancestors after they moved from Romania to Britain. *The Tome of Truth* was written after they fled in the 16th century. They almost lost the instructions, the ceremonies, the rituals, the key to the power behind the bricks." He sat with hunched shoulders.

He seemed smaller. Had he shrunk? Should he even have jumped? But what would they do without him? What would she do? She sank onto the wooden bench as the tram rocked down the track.

"Are these bricks you speak of artifacts? My father told me stories of them, but he acted as though they were fairy tales. I didn't think they really existed." Darlene shook her head. "Are you going to explain any of this to me?"

How much could they tell Darlene, and what did they say? "Darlene, you are of the blood." Did she feel the power in the letter Wilbert wrote to her?

"We'll arrive at the hotel soon." Archie raised an eyebrow as he changed the subject.

"Hmm." Darlene stared out the window as the trees rushed by.

****

The hospital bustled with the voices of nurses and doctors in conversation, and the hush of soft-soled shoes of the nuns. James held the form for Wilbert to sign, then turned away from the head nurse, stumbled, and adjusted Wilbert's arm over his shoulder. The hospital steps that led to Henrietta Street seemed impossible to navigate with Wilbert's weight, but they reached the bottom. A fit of coughing racked Wilbert, and he doubled over.

James pulled out a canteen. "Here." He held it out, and Wilbert drained it. He nodded to James and took a step. James matched his pace, and they crossed the maze of streets and alleys that was Covent Garden.

"Where are you taking me?" He winced as he walked.

"The docks." James wasn't sure if Wilbert was even going to make it to the docks. "You have a boat to catch, remember?"

"Darlene. Is she safe? Is she—" His eyes scanned James' face.

"She's with Sam and Nicole on her way to join her parents. She'll be safe soon and ready to board the steamer. You will too."

"But the ticket?" He patted his pockets. "It's in my room."

"Freddie is bringing it." James stopped. How did he know that? Did Archie put a spell on him somehow, or was this residual Guardian powers? He shook his head. "We're meeting at the White Falcon near the pier."

"I'll need a room."

"It's all taken care of. Let's just concentrate on getting to a tram station and catching the next one."

****

The tram screeched to a stop, and Archie stood. Sam took his arm. His pale complexion tightened the knot in her stomach. She needed him more than ever, and this was killing him. She leaned down and whispered in his ear.

"Are you okay?"

He nodded and stepped down off the tram. Nicole and Darlene waited on the platform for them.

"It's this way." Darlene walked through a light mist as they descended the platform to the street.

The need to hurry had left Sam and Darlene. The whole group followed Darlene as she and Nicole walked ahead. She had the appearance of a young lady of substance. Nicole took in her own attire. Next to Darlene, people must take her for a younger boy cousin, which she was, but where had she gotten that hat?

Darlene scanned the tree-lined street. Was she still worried about Stickel? Sam couldn't blame her. Sam might have enjoyed the views if she weren't so concerned about Archie. Darlene would be with her mother and safe soon.

Sam took Archie's arm. "When will Freddie and Wilbert arrive?"

"Soon. He knows the timeline, and they are following us on the next tram. We will rendezvous at Darlene's hotel."

"Does Daddy know about Wilbert?" Darlene's cheeks brightened with her blush.

"Freddie will get used to the idea, and even though your mother doesn't approve, it is written in the family tree." He shrugged. "So mote it be." Archie coughed, and Sam gripped his arm in hers to keep him steady.

"I can't believe it was Wilbert all this time. It all seems so right, and Daddy will just have to get to know him, then he will love him. Just because he's a bobby does not mean he's not—"

"Good enough?" Nicole scowled at her.

"No one is good enough for me according to my parents, and Mother is so concerned about, well," Darlene's cheeks reddened. "She wants to keep up appearances, but none of that will matter once we get to America." She smiled. "I imagined a life with Graham, but in America, we can live without all this class difference stuff, right?" Her curly hair shook as she picked up her pace.

Archie blinked at Sam, and they followed in silence.

Chapter Thirty-Six

Wilbert sank onto the wooden bench as the streetcar jerked away from the Covent Garden station. James scanned the car, looking for what? Stickel? Archie? The sharp tang of body odor and smoke from the theater fire assaulted his nostrils. He wrinkled his nose and refused to breathe through his mouth, holding his hand to his face.

"I never thanked you." Wilbert began, but started coughing.

"Save your energy. You're still sick." James put a hand on his shoulder. "You'll have time to thank me later." He probably wouldn't, but James didn't care about getting thanked. He cared about getting Sam and Nicole home and stopping Nicole's family names from disappearing.

Archie's spell would take care of Stickel so he could never use the bricks again.

He glanced out the window at the tunnel walls as they rushed through the dark. The train emerged into the light that filled the car. A smattering of rain hit the window.

"I'm exhausted, but excited at the same time." He clasped his hands in his lap and braced his feet on the floor against the rocking of the tram. "You say Darlene got the letter I wrote?"

James nodded. "Yes. She did, but I'm not sure of

anything other than that. You have a long journey ahead, but you can rest once you are on board and regain your strength. The clean, salty air will be good for your lungs."

Wilbert nodded and gave him a small smile, then closed his eyes. James let him sleep. He'd need his energy if he was going to board the boat in the morning because James wouldn't be there to help him.

****

Leo had touched the bricks. It seemed so natural, but had he landed? It was London, Covent Garden, but what was this room? He crouched behind a stack of wooden crates marked with Peebles' Pretties Toy Shoppe. This must be their stockroom.

Was this what Father had tried to explain? The irresistible draw to the artifacts like an inner voice calling him? He'd had no other option but to obey, but it was a voice without sound, more a sensation that he couldn't resist.

He scanned the room. He was supposed to be here for some reason, but what was it? Would Father be glad or mad that he'd used the bricks? If he heard the calling, he must be ready, right? It didn't matter because he was here now.

A rotund, older man lying on the floor opened his eyes. An older woman stood over him, her lipstick running into the wrinkles around her lips. Leo held his position. The man pushed her away and stood. That wasn't very nice. Leo bristled at the crass behavior.

The older man scanned the cellar. "Where is she?"

This must be Charles Mortimer Stickel, Esq. A tremor ran the length of Leo's body. He was here to stop this man.

227

"She's gone, and you are done. Finished." Betty shook a fist at him.

"Gone? Finished? Not as I live and breathe." Mr. Stickel stomped toward the steps.

Betty grabbed at his jacket. "Where do you think you're going?"

He pushed her hands away as she tried to clasp his arm. "I'm through with you. I ask you to do one little thing—"

Leo blinked. Stickel was selfish and mean, and he had to stop him somehow.

"Look." Betty pointed at the stack of crates.

"What?" Mr. Stickel stomped over to where Leo hid. "Hugh?"

Leo leapt onto Mr. Stickel, knocking him to the ground. He knelt on Stickel's back and tied his hands behind the older man with twine.

"Oof. What's the meaning of this? Get off me, Hugh." Mr. Stickel rolled onto his bottom and sat on the floor.

"I'm not Hugh." Leo stood before Mr. Stickel, his arms crossed over his chest.

"Archie?" Stickel tugged to free his hands, but the rope held. "I'm bleeding, you oaf."

"Oh my." Betty sank to the floor in a faint.

Leo stood and glared at Mr. Stickel. A sound on the stairs sent him back behind a shelf filled with wooden puppets and colorful pull toys. He peered between a row of wooden ducks at two men.

Hugh stepped into the cellar with Freddie holding one of Hugh's arms behind his back. "Don't anyone move." Freddie twisted Hugh's arm tighter before letting go. "Uncle Charles." He ground out the words between gritted teeth. "Don't get any ideas."

"He made me do it." Hugh pointed at Stickel.

"You did it for the money I promised you." Stickel rolled to his knees and stood.

Hugh shook his head. "I didn't mean to hurt her. Darlene is my friend." He began to sniffle.

"What kind of friend are you?" Freddie scanned the cellar. "Where is she? Darlene?" He dragged Hugh with him as he checked behind a shelf. "I know you have her."

Mr. Stickel turned his face toward Freddie, then burst into a cackle of laughter. "You're too late. She's gone, and your bloodline ends here. It's the least I can do to salvage my lost money. Unless you want to make a deal—"

Leo waited frozen in position behind the shelves. He couldn't reveal himself yet. Freddie had no idea he even existed.

Betty moaned from the floor. Freddie rushed to her side.

"You always were a do-gooder," Mr. Stickel scoffed, pushing his hands deep into his pants pockets. "That's what got us here in the first place."

"How could you help him hurt my daughter?" Freddie took her collar in his fists. "You were her nurse, for God's sake." He shook Betty by the collar of her dress as she blubbered into her hands.

Stickel brushed the dust from his pants. "So, tell me, Freddie. How much money will it take to get Darlene back?" He rocked on his heels.

Betty sat on the floor in a dusty heap of dress and jacket, her hair mussed and flying around her pudgy face. "Charles, stop it. If Archie has your daughter, the jig is up." She lifted a hand to Freddie. "Darlene should be with your wife by now."

"No, you don't believe that, do you?" Stickel held up his hands. He'd gotten free.

Freddie's gaze shifted as Stickel pushed him. Freddie fell to the floor.

Leo wrung his hands. That didn't go to plan. Father was going to kill him. He had to go. Now. He placed a hand on the bricks.

****

James scanned the platform for Archie and the girls, but they were nowhere to be seen. He took Wilbert's elbow and helped him off the tram and onto the platform.

"Where are they?" Wilbert broke into a coughing fit, and James guided him to a bench, then jogged down the platform.

"They must have gone straight to the hotel." He spotted a luggage cart and jogged over to it, pulling it over to Wilbert.

"Sit on this. I'll get you down to street level at least." He helped the young man onto the wooden cart then pulled it down a ramp to the street. "We have plenty of time, right? The boat doesn't leave until the afternoon tide tomorrow."

"That's correct." Wilbert's eyes glistened, or were they running from the smoke still?

James inhaled the salty air filling his lungs as he stood for a moment, catching his bearings. Trees lined the street and cast shadows across the road. The Thames flowed on the opposite side in a wide expanse of milk-chocolate-colored water. "Which way do we go?"

"Where to, Wilbert? Do you know the waterfront well?"

"Yes." He pointed to the right. "We go several

blocks that direction. The hotel is on the left." He sighed and lay back onto the wooden bed, smooth from years of hauling bags and trunks. "But I'll never make it on foot, and we can't take the cart from the station."

James put a hand on his shoulder. "Isn't that a hansom cab?"

Wilbert raised his head. "It is."

James waved his hand, and a cab whizzed past with a load of noisy passengers. Another cab soon appeared and stopped in front of them.

James helped Wilbert off the cart. "Up you go."

Wilbert leaned heavily on his arm. "We're traveling to the hotel in style." He scooted onto the leather-cushioned seat.

James climbed in beside him. Wilbert grunted in pain as the cab tipped, then righted itself as he sat. "Damn that Stickel. He nearly killed you."

Wilbert coughed, unable to catch his breath from laughing. "It takes more than a madman to kill Wilbert Gordon Smythe?"

"G?" This really is G. James rubbed Wilbert's back. Archie had the herbal concoctions, but he should have carried a dose to ease the coughing at least.

Wilbert grabbed the window ledge of the cab as it lurched forward.

The cabbie glanced over his shoulder. "Where to, guvna?"

"The White Falcon." Wilbert's words rasped from his throat.

"Huh?" The driver scratched his head.

James repeated the hotel name, and the driver clucked the horse into a trot.

Chapter Thirty-Seven

The White Falcon Hotel had been a showplace in its time, but now it showed its age. Still, Sam had to admit, the curtains held their regal swag, and she took in the grandeur of the marble floors that shone under sparkling chandeliers. She raised a hand to Darlene, who scampered up the formal staircase.

Sam ascended the grand staircase with Archie and Nicole, but they stopped on the landing. Darlene had to do this part on her own, but Nicole insisted on making sure she made it to her room. Darlene paused and glanced back, then knocked on a door. Sam's skin tightened around her eyes, and she reached a hand to rub away the tension. Archie blinked at her.

Nicole started. "Did he just blink? Is that the 'all is well' sign?"

A woman with auburn hair going silver at the temples peered out into the hall.

"Mother." Darlene stood with her hands hanging at her sides.

Was she going to try to explain where she'd been? Had her mother missed her?

"There you are. One last petite-quatre before we sail tomorrow? You little scamp—" Mrs. Constance Meyer took her daughter's hand and led her into the room.

The rest of her words were cut off as she pulled the portal shut. Sam peered over Archie's shoulder. Had

Darlene's mother suspected anything? It didn't seem like she had.

"Is that it? Are we done now?" Tension built in her shoulders as she waited for Archie to respond. She shook her head. "Darlene is safe now, right?"

Nicole pressed against Sam's shoulder, waiting for Archie to speak.

Archie blinked at her. Sam wanted to shake him by his lapels. All he needed was a good shake, and maybe he'd act less cat and a little more human. She shrugged. "What now?"

"Several things must happen before she is completely safe." Archie took her hand. "Wilbert's lungs were injured in the fire. Your father is assisting him from the hospital to the hotel, but—"

"But—"

Archie waved his hand in the air. Did he just dismiss her? She opened her mouth, but Archie turned and made his way to the graceful curve of the staircase. She hung back as Archie made his slow descent. She had to trust him, but how did he know Darlene might not be okay? He had been correct about everything so far, and he had died saving that letter. That must mean he knows something, right?

She caught up with Archie on the steps. "It's probably a good thing Darlene is on the second floor, in case Stickel shows up."

He stopped. "This is the first floor."

His monotone voice grated on her nerves.

"I'm pretty sure we climbed a flight of stairs, right?"

"The first floor is called the ground floor in European countries. Remember that."

Nicole smirked. "Even I know that."

"Watch it, know-it-all." She took Archie's arm to help him down the rest of the steps.

A tall man with a younger man's arm draped over his shoulder appeared through the front door. Dad?

Wilbert handed his wallet to Dad as they stood at the front desk. Dad spoke for Wilbert, probably checking him in. A sense of completion filled Sam, and she resisted the urge to race to him and hug him.

"Okay." Archie grinned and patted her shoulder. "Now Darlene is safe."

She couldn't take her eyes off her father. He'd done it. Wilbert would go to America and marry Darlene. Nicole and Archie followed her as she made her way to the front desk.

Archie released Nicole's arm and clasped Wilbert's hand. "Darlene is safe."

Wilbert clung to Archie's hand. "Thanks, mate. That's such a relief."

"She's with her mom on the first floor." Nicole beamed at Archie, and he winked at her.

A warmth settled over Sam at Archie's acknowledgment. She and Nicole still had a lot to learn, but Archie was a good teacher.

"Let's finish getting you checked in," Dad said. Wilbert answered the questions of a young man behind the counter.

Archie patted her hand. "I think we can go home now."

****

Freddie sat on the stockroom floor, grunting as he stood. "You're still here, Uncle Charles."

Stickel laughed in his face.

He completely insane? "Do you think you're getting

234

away this time?" Freddie shook his fist at Stickel. "You've lost. The bricks can't help you now."

"Are you sure of that, Lad? Someone has used them recently." Stickel grinned, his eyes roaming around the stockroom.

Freddie shook his head at the man. He was insane and terrifying in his madness. But if he was going to save Darlene, he had to stand up to his uncle once and for all. He turned and helped Betty to her feet. "If you help me put this lunatic in the asylum, I won't press charges against you. Kidnapping is a serious offense. If you don't, you'll be sent to Working Female Pris—"

Betty gasped. "No. I'll tell you everything." She glowered at Stickel. "What did I ever see in him anyway?" She spat on the floor, missing Stickel.

"Do as you will. I'll be fine." Stickel smirked.

"You'll be no such thing. You're headed to Bedlam." Freddie pointed at Stickel. "And as for you," he said, focusing on Hugh, "you will be sent straight to Hollesley Bay if you don't help me stop this man."

The young man shrank and nodded. "I said I would. Please, I'll talk."

The door from the alley crashed open and Freddie turned as several bobbies clambered down the steps into the small stockroom.

"Good, you've arrived." Freddie stepped back, and Stickel backed away from him to a far wall. What was he up to?

Stickel reached out a hand, and Freddie's stomach tied into a knot. What was he reaching for? His mouth went dry as Stickel stretched his arm toward the pulsing glow.

"No." Freddie leapt forward. Freddie grasped for

Stickel's coat sleeve but got only air. Time stood still as Freddie yelled, "Stop him."

Stickel fell toward the wall, and in a flash of light, he disappeared.

****

Sam took Nicole's arm, and they made their way outside into the sunshine.

Nicole leaned on her arm. "Can we go home now?"

"I think so, but—" Sam stopped in mid-sentence.

Darlene's curls bobbed as she pushed through the front doors of the hotel. "I couldn't let you go without saying thank you and giving you a final goodbye. I finally understand some of the things Father's been talking about all these years about the bricks, and the significance of time." She smiled and gave Nicole and Sam a hug. "We won't meet again, not in my lifetime, but I'll never forget you." Then she turned and disappeared through the White Falcon's front doors.

"I won't forget you either." Nicole raised a hand, but Darlene was already gone.

"I hate goodbyes." Sam squeezed Nicole's arm. Archie met them outside. He stopped on the sidewalk and the color drained from his already pale face. "Something has happened."

Nicole lost the color in her cheeks. "What? How can that be? We did everything you said. Darlene is safe, and Wilbert is here, ready to board the ship in the morning."

Sam shook her head.

James joined them. "What's happening?"

"Stickel. He's done something. Maybe used the bricks." Archie stared in Sam's direction without making eye contact.

James wrung his hands. "Are you sure?"

Archie gave a small nod.

"How? Why? Where?" Sam groaned.

"I cannot answer any of your questions now." He bowed his head.

All Sam wanted was to get Nicole home. Then she'd shower off the dust and grime from 1929 London and eat seventeen pizzas, not necessarily in that order. "Then what do we do?"

"To Peebles' Pretties. We must check the bricks." He strode to the edge of the sidewalk and stopped a cab that had just dropped off a large group.

The driver beamed at them. "At your service, folks."

"To Covent Garden and Peebles' Pretties." Archie pulled himself onto the seat, and Sam glanced at Nicole. Nicole shrugged and stepped into the cab. Sam's weariness hung on her like her dirty clothes.

Stickel. They had to stop him once and for all. She climbed up after Dad and willed the horse to go faster.

Chapter Thirty-Eight

Four muscular bobbies stood in the stockroom staring at the wall. Dust rose. As they walked around the shelves and along the wall. "He's gone, Captain."

Freddie rubbed the lump on the back of his head. He moved to the wall and put his hand on the bricks, but they were dull and dusty. How had that fiend activated them this time? He pounded the spot where Stickel had disappeared.

"Now, sir. Take it easy, sir. I'm Captain Whipple, and we're here to help." Whipple scowled at him as though he were the villain.

"You don't understand. He has—"

"He couldn't just disappear, sir." Captain Whipple scowled at him. "He must have snuck out the door in the chaos of our arrival, right? We'll find him."

Freddie shook his head. He glanced at Hugh, who shrank against the shelves with his eyes clamped shut. He turned to Betty, who stood with her mouth open. "He disappeared."

He didn't have time for this. He had a boat to catch, and he had to get to the hotel. Stickel might have gone there.

Freddie put a hand on Betty's arm. "I'm not sure what you saw, Nurse, but I have to agree with the Captain. He must have slipped up the stairs."

She shuffled her feet and, with wide eyes, scanned

Freddie's face and faces of the police officers.

Freddie shook his head again. Stickel had used the bricks, but they weren't glowing now. They must be tied to Sam and Nicole this time.

"Look, Captain, I have a boat to catch, so I must leave for my hotel." Freddie raked his fingers through his hair. "These two have sworn to help by providing testimony against Mr. Charles Mortimer Stickel Esq. I will leave you to your work."

"I understand, but need your statement as well. Sorry, sir." He turned to the other men, "Bigelow. Billings and Riley, you take the boy, Hugh. Webster and Smythe, you take the woman. I'll take your statement, then you can depart." He turned and headed to the stairs behind Freddie. "To the station, men."

Freddie stood, unable to speak. They didn't understand. He had to make sure Darlene was at the hotel, and if she wasn't, he had to find her before Stickel did. He raced up the steps. Maybe Stickel was on the street. How far could the portly older gentleman get? Who was he kidding? Stickel was gone.

****

Peebles' Pretties stood like a colorful cupcake amid shops that resembled burnt biscuits. Sam jumped from the cab before the cab had fully stopped. The door to the cellar stood ajar. Why wasn't it locked? Where was Hugh? The hair on Sam's arm stood on end. Something had happened here. If this were a perfect world, Stickel and Betty were behind bars already. Hugh too, but this world was anything but perfect.

Nicole pushed past her to the door. "Let's go home now."

She inhaled and pushed her fears aside for Nicole,

but she trembled. What could have gone wrong? They should be finished with this mission. They waited for Archie to climb from the cab, then proceeded in single file down the stairs into the cellar.

A movement in the corner caught Sam off guard, and she skidded to a stop. It was a red-headed boy. "Wait. Archie? What's going on here?" Sam's head bobbed from a red-headed Archie to the red-headed boy. Why did they look related?

Archie stepped forward. "Son?"

"Son?" Sam put up a hand to ward off what Archie was saying. "When did this happen?"

Archie cleared his throat. "I'm in my last life. It's a necessity."

"Oh." Sam shook her head and stared at the young boy. "He's your son, which makes him—"

"The next protector. A magic feline who has no business being here." Archie turned his full attention on the young boy, and Sam cringed, glad he wasn't directing that glare at her.

Leo stared at his feet. "I'm sorry, Father. I know I shouldn't be here, but the urge—"

Archie blinked. That was pride on his face. Sam nudged Nicole, who nodded.

Archie finished Leo's sentence. "Was too strong for you to resist, which means you are ready." Archie rushed to his child and pulled him into an embrace.

Sam glanced at Nicole, who stood with her mouth open.

"What is happening right now?" Sam took a step forward as Leo pushed Archie away. Like father, like son. No PDA. "So, this is your son, Leo?"

Archie released Leo and, ignoring Sam, held his son

by his shoulders, forcing him to maintain eye contact.

Archie blinked again. "So, you are saying you're the reason Stickel is in the wind?"

Leo bowed his head and nodded. "I am."

Nicole gasped and clung to a shelf post. "What did he just say? Stickel escaped?

Sam stumbled as Nicole pulled her aside. "Can we just go home already?"

Sam glanced at Archie. "Soon, but first—"

Archie walked to the wall in the stockroom. He pointed to the bricks. "Did you do this, Leo?"

"It just happened, Papa, and seemed like the right thing to do. They began to glow, and I touched them. Next thing I knew, I was here."

Archie raised a hand. "Other than Stickel's disappearance, I am not sensing negative ramifications of Leo's transgression. Darlene is reunited with her parents, and Wilbert is at the hotel ready to board the steamer in the morning. The space-time continuum has returned to its original order." He placed a hand on Leo's head. "You're just learning on the job, so to speak. This is a valuable lesson."

"Thank you, Father." Leo closed his eyes.

Archie took Leo's hand in his. "My precocious child." He glanced at Sam and Nicole. "How would this family like to go home?"

The hair stood on the back of Sam's neck. Family. This had always been about saving Nicole, her friend, her cousin, her family, and they had done it. Granted, Archie had died, and he had a son? That would take a minute.

"I vote for home," Nicole said in a rush.

Sam nodded as she clasped Nicole's hand. Archie

took Sam's other hand. The bricks glowed brighter.

"Leo, you take Nicole's hand." Archie reached for the bricks. "And I'll—"

Chapter Thirty-Nine

Sam choked as the air was sucked out of her lungs, and the scent of lavender and bleach filled her nostrils. Her heart raced. Would she ever get used to that sensation? She landed hard on her bottom and rolled onto her back, then tipped to her side and cracked open her eye. A warm relief filled her body at the sight of the familiar burgundy couch opposite the mahogany table.

"The throne room." She scanned the familiar room as a log crackled in the fireplace.

Nicole plopped on the floor next to Sam and rubbed her eyes. "Are we home? Right time, right place?" Nicole knelt on one knee and wobbled.

"Slow down." Archie shook a finger at Nicole. "What have I told you about moving too quickly after a jump. You should know—"

"Okay, Archie, lay off for a minute." Sam shook her head at him, but she couldn't stop the grin of relief from forming on her lips.

The question remained, though. Had they stopped Stickel for good, or had he escaped again? She rolled her shoulders. Did it matter? What could he do without an artifact?

Nicole reached out her hand, and Sam pulled her to her feet. "So, Cuz." Nicole grinned from ear to ear.

Sam gave her a smile and leaned against the huge mahogany table. "So, if we're related, I guess this explains why the bricks worked for you in Portland."

Nicole shrugged. "We knew nothing about artifacts or bricks in Portland."

"Why did you touch them this time, though?"

Nicole stared at her feet before answering. She glanced up, her eyes large and watery. "Mom was gone. I could feel it. Then you left to talk to your dad, and I felt a tug, like the bricks were calling me to touch them."

"Well, that tracks." Sam crossed her arms over her chest. "That's how I felt in the Seattle underground."

Leo stepped forward. "I felt that same tug."

Archie cleared his throat and jammed his hands in his pockets. "Yes. The bricks respond when the need arises. Your using the bricks in the Seattle underground is what prompted the bricks to skip James."

"What about me?" James trotted down the stairs and into the throne room. "Am I old news now?" He glanced from Leo to Nicole then to Archie.

"The mistress knew the bricks were responding to Sam, but not to Nicole as well. She knew they were bypassing you, James, and that Sam would become the new Guardian, just as Leo will become the next protector." Archie walked to the couch and sat perched on the edge of a cushion.

"Will Nicole join Sam and me in mandatory training sessions?" Leo sat cross-legged in front of the fireplace.

"What? Why?" Nicole turned to stare at Archie.

"Everyone needs help, right, son?" He patted Leo on the back.

Nicole raised an eyebrow and glanced at Sam.

Sam inhaled and the scent of lavender filled her nostrils. She met Nicole's eyes, but her shoulders tightened, and she wanted to—

Wanted to what? Lavender was her world now. It was all lavender and time. She leaned back against the table. "When do we begin our training?"

"We'll give you all a couple days to rest. Then we'll start with the contents of the vault, their meanings and uses."

Nicole pushed loose hairs behind her ear. "Tomorrow is great. Because I need a shower, like right now, and I should let my mom—"

She stopped and locked eyes with Sam. Sam shrugged.

"If it helps, we've jumped back to the evening of the same day you first jumped, so she won't be missing you yet." Archie put his hands on his hips. "You'll find her in your kitchen."

Sam shook her head. "But so much has happened, and—"

"Maybe that's where we should begin, the element of time." Archie closed his eyes. "But not until tomorrow."

Nicole took a step toward the stairs. "At least we'll know what we're doing next time we jump, and we'll have each other."

"We've always had each other, and that's what saved us in Portland and in London." Sam raked her fingers through her hair. "I'm just glad I don't have to be Guardian alone like Aunt Eli and that we have two Protectors, Archie and Leo."

Leo chuckled and Nicole joined him.

"Kids." Sam beamed at her friends.

Chapter Forty

Sam walked across the grass and down a path to Aunt Eli's spot in Mount Pleasant, thankful the cemetery was located within walking distance of her house. It calmed her jagged nerves to walk here every day, especially since London. She sit with Aunt Eli and talk over what she'd do better next time.

She stood on the south side of the columbarium where Aunt Eli's urn had been interred. She sank to the ground and rested her back against the building, staring into the blue sky. Aunt Eli would have loved this view of Mt. Rainier.

She laid a dusty pink rose on the ground beside her. "We got a new cat." Sam grinned. Aunt Eli would have loved a kitten in the house.

A shadow blocked the sun, and she peered up.

"Father sent me," said a young man with copper-penny red hair, his hands clasped in front of him.

She jumped to her feet. "Leo."

He tilted his head to one side. "Please forgive me. I didn't mean to startle you." He put his hand on the nameplate. "Is this Aunt Eli's resting place? She saved the bricks even after her daughter disappeared. She has her chapter in *The History and Knowledge of the Artifacts*." He was respectful if nothing else.

Sam gave him a small smile. "Yes. Her ashes rest here, but you must know how fierce and brave she was, all the things that I wish I was." She'd wanted more time alone to process today's lesson. Archie was drilling them harder each day.

"But you are those things. I've seen it, and my father says you are perf—" He stopped himself and took a step forward, his hands outstretched. His flood-water pants and his tight t-shirt made her put a hand to her mouth to stop the laughter that threatened to bubble up.

She pointed to the hem of his pants. "Time for another trip to the secondhand store. I'm surprised Mom hasn't taken you already."

Mom had developed a soft spot for the young man. She'd even accepted that he was a magical cat. Sam almost choked when Mom had joined Archie's school of all things artifact, but she'd learned more in the last week about the history of the bricks, the link between the artifacts, and the *Tome of Truth* than Sam had in the last year. Sam shook her head. Having Mom and Nicole on the team, along with Leo, was a real game changer.

She stared at Leo. "Are you ready?"

Leo bowed his head and shuffled his feet. "For what?" He smirked. "I shift from cat to human in the blink of an eye. Turns out I'm hard-wired with information. I know what to do when it comes to the bricks and the artifacts."

"Of course you do." She gazed out over the rolling hills of grass. He was right. He had used the bricks and saved them all from Stickel, even if he'd let Stickel escape.

Leo stepped to the wall and placed his hand on Aunt Eli's marker stone. The cool white marble was striped with a gray vein, and the black lettering stood out in bold relief. He bowed his head. "I also know that you will be one of the greatest Guardians of all time. I'm happy to be on your team as the next Protector."

Greatest Guardian ever? Was she ready for this? She pressed her shoulders back and down. What was it Archie had told her? Fake it until you make it?

"You know that Archie is the Protector, and nothing is going to happen to him for a long time, right? At least not in my lifetime." She rose with her fists clenched by her sides. She wouldn't lose Archie. He'd proven himself a friend in so many ways over the last week. She trusted him. "I accept my fate. I understand the importance of our work now, and I won't shirk my duties, but I can't lose Archie. He's—"

Leo turned to her, his amber eyes unblinking.

"He's my father, and I don't want to lose him either." The crisp fall breeze blew across the cemetery, and billowy clouds rolled across a deep blue sky. He bowed his head. "I didn't mean to frighten you, but I hope you will learn to trust me as well."

Sam sighed. Leo was learning faster than she and Nicole combined. Had Archie sent him to say these things? She wasn't afraid of the bricks anymore, but she still didn't fully trust that they would work the way she wanted them to. It up to her to learn though, right? Each situation would require some new knowledge on how to use the bricks to correct whatever issue was disrupting the time-space continuum.

Leo's face beamed at her, but he didn't blink.

Archie marched across the cemetery and stopped before Aunt Eli's grave. He mumbled some words and closed his eyes, then turned to Leo. "Did you tell her?"

"What's up?" The hair on the back of her neck stood on end. "Why are you here?"

Leo frowned. "We found Stickel. He has found another artifact."

Sam braced herself against the wall with a hand. "So soon? That man is pure evil."

Archie blinked once and nodded. "He is insane, and unfortunately, he has activated the bricks once again. This time near Naples, Italy. We must act fast. Sorry Sam, but we must double your training." He gave her a curt nod, turned, and marched back to the Volvo. Leo ran to catch up to his father.

Dad waved from the driver's seat. She waved back. Would he take the back seat on this next adventure?

Sam turned to the wall and placed her palm on Aunt Eli's headstone. "We were not done with you, you know, but I guess the Universe had other plans." She heaved a sigh and placed her hand over her heart. "I vow to continue our family legacy and guard the artifacts and bricks with my life if I must, but I do it for you."

She closed her eyes and bowed her head. The Puget Sound spread out before her, dotted with sailboats, the snow-covered Olympic Mountains rimming the western skyline. She straightened her spine and lifted her hand to her heart. "Thank you."

Dad honked, and she turned to the waiting car. Maybe this time, they could stop Stickel once and for all.

A word about the author...

Avis M. Adams lives and writes in Portland, Oregon. Her genres include young adult novels, poetry, memoir, and romance. She teaches English at Green River College and is a proud member of the Flamingo's Reborn Critique group. She is an active member of the Pacific Northwest Writers Association and the Willamette Writers, and volunteers at the WW Brown Bag Lunch series. She loves to share sessions on writing craft at local conferences and writer meetings.

The Disappearing Bloodline, a YA time-travel/adventure is her fifth book released by The Wild Rose Press. *The Incident, The Disappearing Names, and The Consequences*, also YA novels, and *The Christmas Wish Knotts*, a romance novella were also published by TWRP. *Quilcene*, a book of her poems was published by Finishing line Press.

She loves to walk, hike, kayak, garden, travel, read, and spend time with family, especially her beautiful granddaughter.

www.ingramcontent.com/pod-product-compliance
Lightning Source LLC
Chambersburg PA
CBHW052028020726
47501CB00004B/1305